ALIETTE DE BODARD

THE TEA MASTER AND
THE DETECTIVE

ALSO BY ALIETTE DE BODARD

OBSIDIAN AND BLOOD
*Servant of the Underworld**
*Harbinger of the Storm**
*Master of the House of Darts**

DOMINION OF THE FALLEN
The House of Shattered Wings
The House of Binding Thorns

XUYA UNIVERSE
On a Red Station, Drifting
*The Citadel of Weeping Pearls**
*The Tea Master and the Detective^*

SHORT FICTION
Of Books, and Earth, and Courtship

* available as a JABberwocky ebook worldwide
^ available as a JABberwocky ebook outside of North America

ALIETTE DE BODARD

THE TEA MASTER AND THE DETECTIVE

Published by JABberwocky Literary Agency, Inc.

The Tea Master and the Detective
by Aliette de Bodard

Cover art © 2018 by Dirk Berger

www.awfulagent.com/ebooks

ISBN 978-1-625674-06-7

The new client sat in the chair reserved for customers, levelly gazing at *The Shadow's Child*—hands apart, legs crossed under the jade-green fabric of her tunic. The tunic itself had been high-quality once, displaying elegant, coordinated patterns, but it was patched, and the patterns were five years old at least, the stuff that got laughed at even in a provincial backwater such as the Scattered Pearls belt. Her skin was dark, her nose aquiline. When she spoke, her accent was flawlessly Inner Habitats. "My name is Long Chau. You have a good reputation as a brewer of serenity. I want to use your services."

The Shadow's Child stifled a bitter laugh. Whatever her

reputation was, it hadn't translated into customers fighting to see her. "Go ahead."

That gaze again from Long Chau. *The Shadow's Child* was used to respect or fear; to downcast eyes; to awkwardness, even, with people who weren't used to dealing with a shipmind, especially one that wasn't involved in passenger service.

The Shadow's Child's body—the metal hull that encased her heartroom and her core—was far away from the office compartment they were both in. The avatar she projected into the habitat wasn't much different from it: a large, sweeping mass of metal and optics that took up most of the office, shifting between different angles on the hull and ports, giving people a glimpse of what she was really like—vast enough to transport merchant crews and supplies, the whole of her hanging in the cool vacuum of space outside the orbitals of the Scattered Pearls belt, with bots crowding her hulls and sensors constantly bombarded by particles. She could have made herself small and unthreatening. She could have hovered over people's shoulders like a pet or a children's toy, as was the fashion amongst the older shipminds. But she'd lived through a war, an uprising and a famine, and she was done with diminishing herself to spare the feelings of others.

Long Chau said, "I'm going into deep spaces to recover something. I need you to make a blend that keeps me functional."

Now that was surprising. "Most of my customers

prefer oblivion when they travel between the stars," *The Shadow's Child* said.

A snort from Long Chau. "I'm not a drugged fool."

Or a fool at all. The name she'd given, Long Chau, was an improbable confection of syllables, a style name, except as style names went it was utterly unsubtle. *Dragon Pearl*. "But you're drugged, aren't you?" *The Shadow's Child* asked. She kept her voice gentle, at that tricky balance point where customers had trust, but no fear.

An expansive shrug from Long Chau. "Of course I'm drugged." She didn't offer further explanation, but *The Shadow's Child* saw the way she held herself. She was languid and cool, seemingly in utter control, but that particular stillness was that of a spring wound so tight it'd snap.

"May I?" *The Shadow's Child* asked, drifting closer and calling up the bots. She wasn't physically there, but physical presence was mostly overrated: the bots moved as easily as the ones onboard her real body.

Long Chau didn't even flinch as they climbed up her face. Two of them settled at the corner of her eyes, two at the edge of her lips, and a host clung to the thick mane of her hair. Most people, for all their familiarity with bots, would have recoiled.

A human heartbeat, two: data flowed back to *The Shadow's Child*, thick and fast. She sorted it out easily, plotting graphs and discarding the errant measurements in less than the time it took the bots to drop down from Long Chau's head.

She gazed, for a moment, at the thick knot of electrical

impulses in Long Chau's brain, a frenzied and complex dance of neuron activation. For all her computational power, she couldn't hope to hold it all in her thoughts, or even analyse it all, but she'd seen enough patterns to be able to recognise its base parameters.

Long Chau was drugged to the gills, and more: her triggers were all out of balance, too slow at low stimuli and completely wild past a certain threshold. *The Shadow's Child* accessed Long Chau's public records, again. She finally asked a question she usually avoided. "The drugs—did your doctor prescribe these to you?"

Long Chau smiled. "Of course not. You don't need a doctor, these days."

"For some things, maybe you should," *The Shadow's Child* said, more sharply than she intended to.

"You're not one."

"No," *The Shadow's Child* said. "And perhaps not the person who can help you."

"Who said I wanted to be helped?" Long Chau shifted, smiling widely—distantly, serenely amused. "I'm happy with what I've achieved."

"Except that you came to see me."

"Ah. Yes." She shook her head with that same odd languidness. "I do have... an annoying side effect. I'm more focused and faster, but only in a narrow range. Deep spaces are well outside that range."

The Shadow's Child had never dealt very well with dancing around the truth. "What are you talking about? Anxiety? Traumatic reaction?"

"Fuzziness," Long Chau said. "I can't *think* in deep spaces."

It wasn't unusual. Time and space got weird, especially deeper in. It took effort to remain functional. Some people could, some people couldn't. *The Shadow's Child* had had one lieutenant who spent every dive into deep spaces curled up on the bed, whimpering—it had been a hundred years ago, before the brews got developed, before brewers of serenity started doing brisk business on space stations and orbitals, selling teas and brews that made it easier for humans to bear the unknowable space shipminds used to travel faster than light.

"You could stop taking the drugs. It would probably help," *The Shadow's Child* said.

"I could." Long Chau's tone made it clear that she wouldn't even consider it. *The Shadow's Child* thought for a while, reviewing evidence as she did. Long Chau was entirely right. She was no doctor; merely a small-rank brewer of serenity struggling to make ends meet. And she just couldn't afford to ignore a customer.

"I could make a blend that would suit you," *The Shadow's Child* said.

Long Chau smiled. "Good. Go on."

Deep spaces. She hadn't returned to them since the Ten Thousand Flags uprising—since her entire crew died and left her stranded. *The Shadow's Child* hesitated again—a moment only—and said, "I don't want to be responsible for accidents. With all that you have in your body, I'd want to monitor you quite closely after you drink the blend."

"I'll have your bots."

"Bots won't be able to react fast enough, with the time differentials. I want to be with you in deep spaces. And it won't come cheap."

Long Chau was silent for a while, staring at her. At length, she stretched, like a sated cat. "I see." She smiled. "I hadn't thought you'd want to return to deep spaces, even for a price. Not after what happened to you there."

It was like a gut punch. For a brief, startling moment *The Shadow's Child* was hanging, not in a comforting void, but somewhere else, where the stars kept shifting and contorting. The dead bodies of her crew littered her corridors, and the temperature was all wrong, everything pressing and grinding against her hull, a sound like a keening lament, metal pushed past endurance and sensors going dark one after the other, a scream in her ears that was hers, that had always been hers...

"How—" *The Shadow's Child* shifted, showing her full size, a desperate attempt to make Long Chau back away. But Long Chau sat in the chair with a mocking, distant smile, and didn't move. "It's not public, or even easily accessible. You can't possibly have found—"

Long Chau shook her head. Her lips, parted, were as thin as a knife. "It is my business to work out things that other people don't pick up on. As I said—I'm more focused. You hesitated before saying yes."

"Because you're a difficult customer."

"It could have been that. But you kept hesitating afterwards. If you'd simply decided to accommodate a difficult customer, the moment of decision would have been the only time you slowed down. There was something else about this bothering you."

"It was a fraction of one of your heartbeats. Humans don't pick up on this."

"They don't." Nothing ventured, again; no hint that she found the silence awkward or unpleasant.

The Shadow's Child hesitated—again for a bare moment, because what her customers did with her blends was none of her business. But she'd just committed to being in deep spaces again, and that was beyond her short limit of unpleasant surprises for the day. "You haven't told me what you need to find in deep spaces."

Again, that lazy, unsettling smile. "A corpse."

Then again, perhaps she was wrong about the unpleasant surprises.

* * *

The Shadow's Child was putting the finishing touches to a test batch of Long Chau's blend. The sweet, intoxicating smell of honeydreamer saturated the room. Two bots clung to the inside of the teapot, taking samples and comparing them to the simulations' results—almost done…

Someone knocked at the door.

"Go away," *The Shadow's Child* started, and then she saw it was Bao, the woman who collected the rent for the compartment that served as her office and laboratory. Her heart sank. "I'm sorry. I didn't mean to be rude." The rent.

7

It had to be the rent. *The Shadow's Child* had scrapped together everything she could in the last days of the year and barely met the deadline, but there were few rules where the Inner Habitat families were concerned.

"May I?" Bao asked.

The Shadow's Child hesitated, but of course Bao would simply be back, if she said no. Bao was polite and pleasant, but unrelenting—which was why the Western Pavilion Le family, who owned *The Shadow's Child's* compartment, employed her.

"Come in," *The Shadow's Child* said. She and Bao had this uneasy relationship, not quite friendship but almost. Bao had been one of the only people willing to risk renting space to a mindship—someone who needed a compartment to receive visitors in-habitat, but who didn't really live there, physically speaking, whom you couldn't easily intimidate or frighten with a couple of toughs if the rent wasn't paid.

The Shadow's Child had the bots prepare tea, but Bao waved a hand. "I won't be long." She pulled up the same chair Long Chau had settled in, and sat, gazing back at *The Shadow's Child*, cool and collected. Unlike Long Chau, her tunic was the latest fashion. The calligraphied verses, bold and forceful, came from Ngu Hoa Giang, the current darling of the Imperial Court. Bao's face was impeccable, with the peculiar smoothness of successive rejuv treatments—and her bots, instead of riding in her sleeves, hung in a jewelled cascade from both her shoulders, an effect that was all the more striking because Bao wore her hair short, in defiance of all conventions. "This is a business visit, in case you had doubts."

"The rent," *The Shadow's Child* said. "I can pay—"

Bao shook her head. The bots moved, slowly. "You did pay." Her voice was low-pitched, and confident. She picked up the tea from the bots, breathed it in; but didn't drink. She never did, when on business. She always said she'd feel personally implicated if she shared food or drink, though she enjoyed the smell of it.

"Then I don't know why you're here." She didn't mean to be this impolite, but it was out of her before she could think.

Bao sighed. "The Western Pavilion Le own the compartment. There's not much that escapes them. Your revenue—"

"It's good enough," *The Shadow's Child* said. She forced herself to be nonchalant.

"Is it?" Bao's gaze was piercing. "I said business, but perhaps it'd be more accurate to say I'm here as a friend. Or a concerned relative. You may not need much space, or that much money to pay for it—"

If only. She should have had money for her repairs, but everything had gone into making sure she wouldn't find herself homeless. Shipminds such as her were meant to be the centre of families: grown by alchemists in laboratories, borne by human mothers and implanted into the ship-bodies designed for them, they were much longer lived than humans—the repositories of memories and knowledge, the eldest aunts and grandmothers on whom

everyone relied. They were certainly not meant to be pen-
niless and poor, and *The Shadow's Child* would die before
she'd beg from her younger relatives—who were, in any
case, even worse off than her. Their salaries as minor
scholars in the ministries paid them a pittance, and they
could barely afford their own food.

She could have remained as she was, in orbit around
the habitats. But without office space, how could she
practise her trade? No one would take a shuttle to come
onboard a distant shipmind, not when there were closer
and better brewers of serenity available. "I get your point,"
she said. "And I'm grateful, but—" But she didn't need
more stress. She didn't need her niggling worst fears to
be proved right.

Bao pulled back the chair, and rose. "But I'm not good
news? I seldom am." She shrugged. "I know you won't
consider passenger service—"

"No," *The Shadow's Child* said. It was reflex, as if
someone had pushed, hard, on an open wound and she'd
screamed.

"The money is far better. Especially you—you're a
troop transport. You could take on a lot of passengers and
cargo each run." Bao's voice was soft.

"I know."

Bao was smart enough to drop the subject. She
looked at the bookshelves: not physical books, because
The Shadow's Child would have needed to read them
through her bots, but a selection of the ones in her electronic library, displayed in matching editions in a riot

of colours. "I see you have the latest Lao Quy. It's well worth it, if you need a distraction. She's really got to be a master of the form."

Bao and *The Shadow's Child* shared a fondness for epic romances and martial heroes books, the kind of novels scholars looked down on as trash but which sold thousands of copies across the belt. "I haven't started it yet," *The Shadow's Child* said. "But I liked the previous one. Strong chemistry between characters. And to have set it in a small mining operation was a smart change of setting. I loved the mindship and their habitat's Mind lover, trying to find each other after decades had passed."

"Of course you would. She's good," Bao said, fondly. "This one is different. I'd argue better. We can talk about it later, if you want, but I wouldn't want to spoil the experience." She looked at the blend on the stove, and shook her head. "I'm not going to keep you from your customer."

A customer *The Shadow's Child* didn't *like*, but she'd pay handsomely, and—as Bao had all too clearly reminded her—*The Shadow's Child* couldn't afford to be picky.

* * *

The Shadow's Child had to take Long Chau onboard, of course. When Long Chau's footsteps echoed in the corridors of her body, it was an odd and unsettling feeling. She'd taken on a few passengers for the army after Vinh and Hanh and her crew died, but everyone had been so careful with her, as if she were made of glass. And after she'd been discharged she'd refused to take on further passengers.

She had no need of sensors or bots to follow Long Chau's progress through her. The footsteps, slow and steady—each of them a jolt in the vastness of her body—went through room after room, unerringly going towards the cabin she'd set aside for Long Chau. From time to time, a longer pause, feet resting lightly on the floor of rooms, a faint heat spreading outward on her tiles: once, near the seventh bay, staring at the scrolling display of fairytales Mother had brought back from the First Planet; another time at the start of the living quarters, reading the Thu Huong quote on houses being a family's heart—new paint and a new calligraphy, replaced after the ambush. *The Shadow's Child* had had network decoration, once: a wealth of intricate interlocked layers only visible with the proper permissions. But she'd lost everything, and she hadn't seen the point of putting more than basic work into this after she was discharged.

When Long Chau reached the cabin, she found a table and a chair, and a cup of steaming tea set there. She raised her eyes, as if she could see *The Shadow's Child* hovering somewhere above her. It was pointless: everything around her was the ship. All *The Shadow's Child* really needed to do was focus her upper layers of attention on this room, while in the background the bots and everything else continued to run without any input, and the solar wind buffeted her hull as her orbit swung her around the habitats—all familiar sensations that barely impinged.

Long Chau pulled up the chair, settling down into it without any apparent nervousness. Her movements were slow and deliberate. *The Shadow's Child* felt it all. The scraping of the chair, all four feet digging into her floors; Long Chau's weight shifting, lightly pressing down on top of the chair. "You're quite lovely," Long Chau said.

It'd have been a compliment from anyone else. From her, though, said with an utterly impassive face? *The Shadow's Child* couldn't be sure. Not that she should have cared, except that it would affect her relation with a customer. "Your blend is on the table."

A raised eyebrow. "So I've seen." Long Chau considered the cup for a while. *The Shadow's Child*'s bots climbed up onto her face and head again. She let them, without even so much as a reaction. The dense, urgent pattern of her brain activity was now available to *The Shadow's Child*. She'd had enough time now to build a model of what Long Chau considered normal, and nothing there was surprising.

"It's not poisoned." The smell of honeydreamer saturated the room, bringing back, for a brief moment, memories of *The Shadow's Child*'s first disastrous attempt at cooking it, when the bots had failed to remove the carapaces and they had popped in the heat, sending shards flying all over her compartment.

"Of course it's not," Long Chau said, with a hint of annoyance. She raised it to the light, lips slightly parted;

stared for a while longer. "It's fascinating, isn't it, that a few herbs and chemicals can have this effect?"

Hours of poring over Long Chau's metabolism and brain patterns, reconstructing the drugs in her system—trying to find out which compounds would keep her functional, guessing at what she might call "slow thoughts", wondering if the mixture would flat-out short-circuit her neurons, make her suicidal or, more likely, even more reckless and over-confident, with the risk she'd endanger her own life on a whim ... "Are you mocking my work?"

"On the contrary," Long Chau said. Her face was set in a peculiar expression, one *The Shadow's Child* couldn't read. "Merely appreciating the value of localised miracles." She sounded... utterly earnest, in a way that disarmed the angry reply *The Shadow's Child* would have given her.

Silence stretched, long, uncomfortable. *The Shadow's Child* became aware again of her core in the heartroom, of the steady beat that sustained her—pulsing muscles and optics and brain matter, holding her connectors in an unbreakable embrace. One two, one two...

In the cabin, Long Chau appeared utterly unfazed. She merely raised the cup to her lips after a long while, and drank from its thin rim in one long, slow go—didn't even seem to breathe while doing so—and set it down on the table. "Shall we go?"

The Shadow's Child didn't need to move to dive into deep spaces. She'd already asked for permission from

Traffic Harmony, and within deep spaces it wouldn't matter if they overlapped another ship. She watched Long Chau, because it was her job.

A centiday since she'd taken the blend—fifteen outsider minutes—and no visible effect yet. The tea *The Shadow's Child* had given Long Chau was a mix of a downy white Dragon Quills with a stronger, more full-bodied Prosperity Crescent, with fried starvine root and crushed honeydreamer, scattered among the downy leaves. She watched Long Chau's vitals, saw the minute changes to breath and heartbeat. The hands moved a fraction faster as Long Chau got up and stared at the walls—*through* the walls.

"I'm not there," *The Shadow's Child* said.

"You're in the heartroom. I know." Long Chau's voice was mildly irritated. "I'm familiar with shipminds, though I've seldom had the occasion to go into deep spaces."

While she was speaking, *The Shadow's Child* plunged into deep spaces—not far in, just enough on the edge that she could see Long Chau's reactions. "Tell me about the corpse," she said. Around her, the corridors shifted and changed. A faint, trembling sheen like spilled oil spread across the walls, always in the corner of one's eyes. Outside, the same sheen stole across the habitats, the sun and the distant stars—a distorted rainbow of colour that slowly wiped them out. Her hull was awash with faint cold, the brisk flow of stellar wind around her replaced by a faint, continuous pressure. It should have felt like coming home—like a fish diving into a river at the end of a long, breathless interval onshore—but all she could feel within her was tautness, and the rapid beat from her heartroom, everything pulsing and contracting in ways she couldn't control.

It would be fine. She wasn't where it had happened. She wasn't deep in—just at the very edges, just enough to keep Long Chau satisfied. It would be fine.

"You said any corpse would do," she said.

"Of course." Long Chau appeared utterly unfazed by deep spaces. *The Shadow's Child* would have liked that to be a front, but Long Chau's heartbeat, even and slow, said otherwise. "I'm writing a treatise on decomposition. How the human body changes in deep spaces is a shamefully undervalued area of study."

"I can see why you'd be a success at local poetry clubs," *The Shadow's Child* said, wryly.

It didn't seem to faze Long Chau. "I would be, if I had anything to do with them." She looked around her. The walls had caved in now, receding in what seemed a long and profound distance; the table was folding back on itself, showing the metal it had been made from, the bots that had hammered it into shape—the broken scraps of what it'd be, when it finally broke down, every moment existing tightly folded on top of one another. "How deep are we?"

Two centidays since she'd taken the blend. She seemed fine. Unfair. Heartbeat normal, veins slightly dilated but not past the expected top of the range, pupil constriction slowly easing up—the activity map almost a match for when she'd sat in *The Shadow's Child*'s office. *The Shadow's Child* tried to calm herself down. She stretched her core in the heartroom, slowly and deliberately, away from Long Chau's prying eyes. A good thing she hadn't boosted up the arrogance: it was an easy way to keep people functional in deep spaces if they had enough self-confidence to start with, but she didn't think she could have borne the result for long.

"Not very deep," *The Shadow's Child* said. "I'd rather keep you in safe areas." It was untrue.

"And yourself from unpleasant memories," Long Chau said. "It makes sense." And then, with an odd expression in her voice, "You're not recovered. Even being here makes you nauseous."

"Shipminds don't get nausea," *The Shadow's Child* said. It was a lie—especially now, with no distance between her body and herself, she felt rocked by alternating waves of warmth and cold, her core coming apart in ten thousand pieces in the heartroom. She forced herself to be calm. "And you have no idea what you're talking about. You're guessing."

"I don't guess." Long Chau's voice was curt. "You were in an accident during the uprising. A mission gone bad because of lack of information. Something that badly crippled you, and left you in deep spaces for some time."

She—she'd hung around in places where nothing made sense anymore, with no one alive onboard anymore. The crew was gone, and Captain Vinh was lying curled just outside the heartroom, her hands slowly uncurling as death took hold. Nothing but the sound of her panicked heartbeat, rising and rising through empty corridors and cabin rooms until it seemed to be her whole and only world—she was small and insignificant and she would be forever there, broken and unable to move and forever forgotten, her systems always keeping death at bay...

Long Chau was still speaking, in that same dispassionate tone. As if nothing were wrong, as if she could not feel the chills that ran up and down the corridors, the pressure that was going to squeeze *The Shadow's Child* into bloody shards. "There is no information about you during the uprising, and you're in surprisingly good shape considering your age, and the fact that you're barely scraping by earning your living. That means either a wealthy family—but you don't have the accents of wealth—or that the military shouldered your maintenance until a few years ago." Every word hurt—the currents of deep spaces pressing against her hull, again and again, drawing the will to live out of her—but she couldn't commit suicide because everything was offline or broken.

"But you haven't been with the military for the last five years or so. That ugly gash on your hull, just below the painting of the Azure Dragon gardens, is around that age and no one fixed it. Which means you were discharged shortly after the uprising. You're completely traumatised, but showing no other sign of damage. Meaning whatever happened was under the military's watch, and they repaired it for you. So a mission gone wrong."

"I. Am. Not. Traumatised." It felt like swallowing shards of glass. She'd still be there, body non-functional, coms dead, if another mindship hadn't happened to go by and notice a light blinking on her hull—near that painting Long Chau was so casual about.

It had only been a bi-hour or so, in outside time—eight centidays, nothing more—not even the time it took for a banquet, such a pitiful duration to someone like her. Except that, in deep spaces, it had felt so much longer.

"You tiptoe around deep spaces like a mouse around a tiger's claw." A gentle snort from Long Chau. "See. I don't guess."

"You—" *The Shadow's Child* tried to breathe, to say something, anything that wouldn't be a scream. Outside, the currents of deep spaces bathed her—clinging, lightly, to her hull—like hands, awaiting the right moment to curl into claws. "You have no right."

Long Chau looked puzzled, for a moment. "Why not? You asked me to prove it."

"I didn't."

A long, awkward silence. "Oh. My apologies. I thought you'd want to see how I'd come to those deductions."

The Shadow's Child was still shaking. "No. I don't."

"I see." A long, careful look. "I'm sorry. I didn't mean to hurt, but it doesn't change that it did happen." A further silence. Then, "Tell me about the wreck."

A customer. Long Chau was just a customer. And *The Shadow's Child* needed those, no matter how eccentric they might be. She had to remember that—but all she wanted was to drop Long Chau off on the habitat and forget any of this had ever happened. "There is no shortage of wrecks here. *The Three in the Peach Gardens* isn't very far in, and he was carrying passengers when he died."

"How long ago was that?"

"Not during the uprising. Five years ago," *The Shadow's Child* said. She'd picked a ship she hadn't known, not even as a distant acquaintance. She supposed it'd be different, to see a wreck washed by the tides of deep spaces rather than a recent corpse, but she wasn't sure enough of how she would react.

She'd stared at ships' corpses, back then, after the ambush—at twisted, inert metal, at dead optics, at broken hulls, the damaged wrecks all around her, the lucky ones who'd died—knowing that her own damage wasn't severe enough and that she would merely remain trapped, for moments that would stretch to an eternity.

Long Chau laid a hand on the wall. Her touch was a jolt, a small pinpoint of warmth in the vastness of *The Shadow's Child*'s body. "I see. Fresh is better, from my point of view. The older corpses just become unrecognisable." She shook her head. "Not much to work on." And then, looking up once more, "You're not disgusted, are you."

"By what you want?" *The Shadow's Child* forced herself to be casual. "I've seen corpses during the uprising. They don't frighten me."

She moved, slowly and cautiously, among the outer layers of deep spaces with short and controlled motor bursts, keeping the time and space differentials as small as she could—even smaller than she'd done for her passengers, back when she was carrying them. She wasn't sure how Long Chau would react, even if so far everything seemed to be proceeding as expected.

The world rippled and changed. The cold outside her hull became replaced with a touch of that odd, familiar warmth—something that bit deep inside, all the way to her heartroom, a memory of being held and loved, and safe—a centiday after her birth, being carried to the heartroom and safely enclosed there, where nothing could harm her. A memory of herself, slowly stretching tendrils through the connectors, making the ship her body, now and forever. Mother's hands were shaking with weakness, but she didn't falter, and even from far away, even dazed with the shock of breathing in dry, searing air, with the shock of touch after so long in the womb, *The Shadow's Child* felt her absolute determination, her unwavering strength and love.

And then she remembered that this was the place that, but for a quirk of fate, would have forever trapped her, drained and broken beyond healing.

She was safe. She was just on the shallow end of deep spaces. They couldn't harm her.

"Here." *The Shadow's Child* kept her voice steady, and called up the sensors for Long Chau. A viewscreen hung in front of her in the room rather than a straight beam, as she'd not granted Long Chau any implants access.

The Three in the Peach Gardens had been a larger ship

than *The Shadow's Child*. He had survived the wars and the uprising, but not the technical malfunction that had blown the motors and half of his heartroom, cutting off coms. By the time anyone realised what was wrong, the ship was already dead, the passengers struggling to reach shuttles without any of the protections the shipmind had afforded them against the deep spaces. Some of them had made it, but not all.

The wreck was lit with washes of light, as if a child were painting over it, over and over—every few moments the colours slowly shifted, and not in a uniform way, patches of deeper radiance spreading from random areas on the wreck of the hull. Here and there, the light snagged on something: a piece of stray metal, a fragment of glass; the lighter shape of a corpse.

Such a waste. All these lives, extinguished so fast. Her sensors could pick out fragments of jade, implants, teapots and tea cups: too many of them with the same delicate pale green eggshell pattern, they must have been from *The Three in the Peach Gardens*'s personal stores—and his burnt bots, each loss a wound; though he wouldn't have suffered, would he? At least it would have been fast.

At least...

Watch over them, A Di Da—may they reach the Pure Land and be cut free from the cycle of rebirth and pain...

Long Chau watched the screen. Nothing in her expression changed: she might as well have been admiring a painting or a particularly fine poem. "Here," she said, making a gesture with her hands. Bots ran up, clinging to her wrists. She shifted the view with sweeps of her fingers until it settled on a particular shape. "This one."

A middle-aged woman, with loose, mottled skin hanging loose on rib cage and pelvic bone, her shape already compressed into improbable angles by the pressures of unreality around her—she'd had a shadow skin to survive the vacuum of normal space, but of course it wouldn't have survived the plunge into deep spaces: the long, dark tatters of it streamed from her corpse like hair, or threads tying her to an impossibly distant puppet-master.

"Why that one?" A stupid question. She'd said any corpse would do.

Long Chau watched the corpse like a hawk. "Because it's wrong."

"Wrong?"

"You'll see."

Long Chau fell silent, and *The Shadow's Child* wasn't going to give her the satisfaction of asking questions. The sooner she got the corpse the faster they'd get out, and the sooner she'd get paid—though part of her still yearned for the comfort of being *there*, of coming home. She sent her bots out and one of her antiquated escape pods, just large enough that the bots could manoeuvre the corpse into it.

Long Chau watched them intently. "Don't fold her," she said, sharply, as three of the bots started dragging an arm towards the open hatch of the pod. "No, not that way!"

"You're quite free to handle the bots yourself," *The Shadow's Child* snapped.

For a moment she thought Long Chau would ask to. It would have been a headache and a waste of time, as Long Chau's dexterity with bots was far inferior to *The Shadow's Child*, but then she subsided in sullen silence. "Try not to damage her," Long Chau said.

The Shadow's Child opened one of her empty bays. Cold blew in through the open airlock, a wind that seemed to freeze all feeling out of her, followed a moment later by a blast of shrivelling warmth, and a faint sound on the cusp of hearing, like the chittering of a thousand crickets. Colours shifted and played across the walls of the bay—again and again, the pressure subtly changing as they moved. The pod docked with a crunch. She clenched the airlock closed. The pressure differentials slowly smoothed themselves out, and silence spread across the bay. She found her core beating hard and fast, the connectors trembling in her grasp.

Breathe. She could do this.

The bots dragged the corpse out of the pod. Their feet clicked, one by one, on the floor. The corpse was a heavier, harsher weight—not the suppleness of tissues, but something more akin to polished stone, soundlessly scraping against the floors of the bay. *The Shadow's Child* adjusted the temperature downwards to prevent further decomposition. It lay there, staring at the ceiling: its eyes had started to harden into jewels, the cornea looking more like ivory than tissue. The nails had started to bulge outwards—faint drops of blue pearling on their edges, with the dirty rainbow colours of oil spills—and the entire skin had taken on the translucent brittleness of jade.

As Long Chau headed there—still utterly unfazed by the alien traceries of light that deep spaces caused to play on the walls and floor—*The Shadow's Child* reviewed the bots' data.

By the time Long Chau reached the bay, she was thinking, hard.

"We might have a problem," she said, because she didn't want to admit out loud that Long Chau had been right. Her voice echoed in the empty bay, the words *multiplying* for the briefest of moments, shifting into a crooning lullaby. Bleed through. They were drifting in too deep.

Not on her watch.

She nudged her motors into life, started climbing towards the shallows again. The pressure eased. The temperature stabilised again, and there was just that odd light, trembling on every wall and every floor from cabins to heartroom. Her bots felt sluggish, her body too large to contain her thoughts. Exhaustion was creeping in. It shouldn't have, but of course she knew why she was so tired. It was fighting her own treacherous memories that did it.

"Problem? Nothing unexpected." Long Chau knelt by the corpse's side. Her own bots crawled out of her sleeves, legs clicking on the floor before they connected with frozen flesh. She slipped on thin gloves, snapping them onto her long and elegant fingers in a seamless gesture. Her face set again. Her movements became languid and slow again as she lifted one hand, then the other; and then bent over the mottled, loose skin of the face. With the same slow deliberateness she touched the filaments of shadow skin; gathering them in a dark fistful, she examined them with the attention of a scholar piecing together a lost book.

When Long Chau looked up again, her face was utterly expressionless. "Exactly what I thought. That corpse wasn't aboard the ship." It wasn't a question.

"I'm not sure, but—"

Long Chau stretched, slowly, lazily. "Be sure. Given the state of decomposition, the shadow skin held for at least a few days, providing her corpse with air. More, I think. Five years ago, shadow skins were in their infancy, so this means this particular shadow skin would have been unusually efficient, and expensive."

That wasn't the only explanation. "She could have bought that shadow skin herself."

"A woman with nails this short and this damaged? Not unless she'd recently become wealthy and invested in one. And she could afford travel aboard a mindship. Possible but very unlikely," Long Chau said. She didn't look at the corpse again—everything she recited, she obviously did from memory, her tone taking on the sharp cadences of a school master. "She didn't have rejuv treatments. You can see it on the skin. Rejuved skin clings to bones, even after bloating. She was in manual labour. Her wrists bear the repetitive strain of controlling bots with her hands, which means she couldn't afford implants, or was in an occupation where hands were more convenient. Mining, or possibly orbital maintenance—the fields there tend to interfere with implant technology. No one in those fields makes money, or remains in them."

All compelling arguments, but surely there had to be a flaw in them. "She might have been doing this out of passion."

Long Chau snorted. "Shortening your life for menial, ill-considered and ill-paid work? Possible, but improbable."

"So what?"

"So she wasn't on board the ship. I'd say she died a year ago, perhaps? At most. I don't have enough samples of corpses in deep spaces to compare. That was supposed to be the point of this expedition." She sounded annoyed again, as if the corpse had personally offended her.

"What did she die of?" The conversation was now flowing effortlessly; and *The Shadow's Child* was more curious than she'd have liked to admit.

"I don't know," Long Chau said. "It was a long way away from here—the currents of unreality carried her a long way: you can see it in the way the shadow skin got shredded. And I could speculate, but it's an unhealthy pastime. We need certainty, not smokescreens."

"How—" *The Shadow's Child* started, stopped. "How did you know? She was too far away. You can't have seen it."

"She stood out," Long Chau said. "It was obvious, and

would have been to you as well—but you let emotion get in the way of simple observation."

"Emotion?" *The Shadow's Child* breathed, feeling her heartroom constrict around her. She wouldn't achieve anything if she got angry.

"You felt sorry for the mindship."

"Don't cheapen it."

"I'm not. There is a time and place for everything, and this was neither," Long Chau said, curtly. A pause, then, in a different tone: "I was right."

"In general?" *The Shadow's Child* didn't bother to keep the sarcasm out of her voice.

Long Chau shook her head. "You *are* very good at what you do." She turned away from the body, as if closing a door in a mental space somewhere. "I can think almost as well as if I were on-habitat."

Almost better, in fact, if *The Shadow's Child* had to guess. Her current activity map, all lit up, was certainly suggestive. "Thank you." She tried very hard to make it sound sincere, even though she didn't want to be polite, or *kind*, to Long Chau—not after what she'd done. "What now? We should contact the magistrate—"

"Of course," Long Chau said. "I wouldn't dream of obstructing the Empire's justice." Something in the way she moved, in the way she stood, caught *The Shadow Child*'s attention. Her profile was the lean and sharp one of a tiger on the prowl suddenly sighting prey. "But I'd like to make a few inquiries of my own in parallel."

"Inquiries?"

"You never did ask me what I did for a living."

"Because it was hardly relevant!"

She'd expected a quick, amused glance upwards, but Long Chau didn't even blink. "I'm a consulting detective."

"A what?"

"An adviser," Long Chau said. "A solver of people's problems, especially when such problems involve lawsuits and magistrates."

A consulting detective. So many thoughts pressed themselves in *The Shadow's Child* that she was hard-pressed to pick one. "You really think you can do better than the magistrate to find out how that woman died?"

"I *know* I can." It'd have been unbelievably conceited, but Long Chau's voice was completely emotionless: it was a statement of fact, and not even one she took particular pride in. "Even if I weren't smarter than the magistrate, the tribunal is overwhelmed and understaffed, and unlikely to expend much energy trying to solve a nameless woman's death."

"I don't understand why you would bother," *The Shadow's Child* said. "No one is going to pay you anything for this."

This time Long Chau did smile, and it seemed to illuminate her entire face. "Why? Because I can."

* * *

They dropped off the body to the magistrate's tribunal—rundown and overflowing with clerks so harried they gave them a cursory interview, promising them to be in touch and obviously lying about it. It all proved Long Chau—infuriatingly—right again. She wasn't smug about it. Fortunately, or it'd have crossed the line from annoying to unbearable once again.

When *The Shadow's Child* got back to her small office, she saw that Long Chau had paid her for the blend. She hadn't expected Long Chau to be that fast, but she wasn't about to complain. She put the money aside in her account, earmarking it for the rent; and, after a brief hesitation, granted Bao viewing access to the transaction. It wasn't enough to cover the rent, but it was a good enough sum: it should reassure Bao and the Western Pavilion Le that *The Shadow's Child*'s business was broadly profitable.

Then she settled down to research. Not the corpse or its history—as, no doubt, Long Chau was doing. She had little doubt Long Chau would be back; and she wasn't sure what she wanted to do, if that happened.

One thing she did know. She didn't intend to be defenceless. If Long Chau could effortlessly pry into her past, then *The Shadow's Child* could pry into hers.

It was much harder.

Her name was a style name, that much was certain—except that it appeared to be used, insofar as *The Shadow's Child* could determine, only for treatises on utterly obscure subjects, ranging from the evolution of bruises in the vacuum to the effects of certain substances on creativity. The face itself, run through the hours of recordings on the habitats, didn't appear to evoke anything unusual, except that Long Chau, as expected, didn't have much of a social life: no sightings in poetry clubs or tea houses. Her compartment was in the same habitat as *The Shadow's Child*, but not as well placed, the network there sluggish. Her bots were the older kind: slow, and requiring a lot of attention to be commanded.

On her past, there was nothing. Long Chau had sprung into activity six years ago, shortly after the uprising. But before that, nothing. Her accent and demeanour were those of scholars—not only that, but of one used to power. Most likely? A missing scion of an Inner Habitat family, playing at poverty while still supported by her family's money.

All the checks on that came back negative. There were a handful of rebel children from the Inner Habitats, but all much younger than Long Chau. A minor scion from a numbered planet, closer to the centre of the Empire? She wasn't nearly high-handed enough for that.

Consulting detective.

The Shadow's Child would have dug deeper—never minding that her time would have been better spent trying to gain customers rather than pointlessly obsessing about one. Her only obligation was in a few days: a dinner with two of her relatives, Dieu and An Giang—faraway descendants of Mother who always had hilarious anecdotes about their times in the ministries of the Scattered Pearls belt. But *Sharpening Steel into Needles* intervened.

In the small shipmind community, *Sharpening Steel*

into Needles was a living legend. They were one of the eldest ships in the Scattered Pearls belt, who remembered a time when the Empire had been so small the planets didn't need to be numbered or classified. And they knew exactly what they wanted, and didn't let anyone's objections stand in their way for long.

"You can't remain cooped up in this office for long," *Sharpening Steel into Needles* said. "Come, let's have a tea together."

The Shadow's Child put up a brave but doomed front. "I'm not really here. I'm in space."

"That's a trivial part of you. The majority of your processing powers are in the habitat," they said.

To her surprise, *Sharpening Steel into Needles* took her, not to a teahouse, but to their own compartment: a riot of colours and display cabinets filled with fine porcelain. Their own hobby was collecting rare pieces, and several of the bowls were exact replicas of ones used in ceremonials at the Imperial Court, made in the exact same workshops. The cabinets were interspersed with holos of space: the overlay *Sharpening Steel into Needles* reserved for other shipminds, though *The Shadow's Child* had a suspicion the other ship had removed all the vids and paintings involving deep spaces. She'd have been embarrassed at needing to be taken care of, but just the thought of deep spaces was enough to make her core clench.

On the low table was an overlay of various dishes from caramel pork to noodle soup, and green tea the colour of verdigris. None of it was real, and neither of them ate, per se, but food for them was memories—of feasts and places and people, accumulated and refined through the centuries of their lives.

The Shadow's Child picked at the caramel pork. For a brief moment she was a child again, watching fireworks go off in the habitat, and she fell asleep curled up in Mother's lap. And then the memory passed, and she was an adult again, her human parents since long ashes.

"You've been making inquiries," *Sharpening Steel into Needles* said.

"There's nothing wrong with that."

A pause, then, "You're angry."

"I'm not."

"Don't be unreasonable, child." *Sharpening Steel into Needles* sounded amused. "That one annoys everyone."

"Long Chau? You know her?"

"Not I, no. But a few of the younger shipminds. None of them in your—ah. Line of work."

They disapproved, though of course they would never put it in so many words: they thought shipminds should serve the Empire and not seek to profit.

As if there was much profit in brewing blends for humans.

The Shadow's Child thought for a while, trying to keep her feelings leashed. "These other ships—"

"Yes?"

"Do they know who she is?"

Sharpening Steel into Needles shifted closer. Their avatar was small and perfectly formed, hovering over the table—the sharp, flowing designs of the Empire centuries ago. "They were referred to her by an agency. She has quite a reputation by now."

"But no life—"

"Before the uprising? No. Why do you want to know? Surely your business with her is finished."

"We—we found a body," *The Shadow's Child* said. "A woman who died in deep spaces."

"And you have some sympathy. That's understandable."

"*She* has none." And then she realised what she'd said and fell silent, horrified. Because it wasn't true. True, Long Chau had never shown any emotion. But she'd never called the corpse "it", always "she". And of course she might think the death an abstract problem to be solved, but she was looking into it, all the same. And—before she'd started dissecting *The Shadow's Child*'s past, she'd been trying, however awkwardly, to show consideration, to check that *The Shadow's Child* was doing fine in deep spaces. "I don't know what to think of her."

"She fascinates you?"

The Shadow's Child wanted to say no, but it would have been a lie. Long Chau was an expanding star, burning loud and bright, mesmerising in her relentlessness, and ultimately one that would swallow you whole.

Sharpening Steel into Needles was very still, watchful. Their bots were perched on the porcelain bowls in the display cases, all sensors turned towards *The Shadow's Child*. *Sharpening Steel into Needles* was going to take that opportunity for a tongue-lashing rebuke, words that had reduced other ships to weeping. But when they spoke, their voice was slow, thoughtful. "She's not an outsider to the belt. In every interaction she had with other ships, she was very cognisant of families and customs that most outsiders never grasp."

"She's a fast learner," *The Shadow's Child* said.

"Not that fast. Don't make the mistake of granting her magical powers." A pause, then, "*Pomegranates Buried in Sand* thinks—and I'm inclined to agree—that she's too familiar with the tribunal."

"Surely, as a detective—"

"Not that kind of familiarity," they said. "She was arrested, at some point. I've seen the other ships' vids of her. The scans show scars on both her arms, in a pattern that's characteristic of militia bots."

So not only arrested, but interrogated under mind-probe drugs. "Is that the reason—"

"That she keeps drugging herself? You'd have to ask her."

She'd almost have felt sorry for Long Chau, if she didn't remember the casual arrogance and high-handedness with which she'd acted throughout.

"What will you do, if you find out who she is?" *Sharpening Steel into Needles* asked.

She'd never quite stopped to consider. Would she really throw Long Chau's past at her, with the same casual lack of consideration? "I—" she started, then stopped. "She'll be back."

"Of course. She attacks problems the same way

crocodiles attack prey, with relentless abandon. Giving up would be physically painful." They sounded amused again.

The Shadow's Child reached for rice. She inhaled the fragrance, thinking of a kitchen filled with the laughter of children. "I don't know what I'll do. I just—"

"Need to know?" A silence. Then, "Control. It's a currency you've always been short of."

"Don't." She'd see them again, if *Sharpening Steel into Needles* insisted—all of her living and her dead, Captain Vinh and Lieutenant Hanh and all the ones who'd thought they knew better than her, that a ship didn't need to know the larger picture—that had led her, inescapably, into the ambush—and from there to hang, wounded and broken, in the deepest places, where time kept stretching and snapping, like claws drawn again and again against her hull. "Please don't."

This time, there was pity in their voice. "I won't."

* * *

The Shadow's Child was in the middle of a tricky assessment on an Outer Habitats bots-handler when Long Chau walked into her office.

"We need to talk," she said. "When convenient."

The Shadow's Child pointedly didn't move. "It's not."

"We need to talk all the same." Long Chau lounged against the wall with the ease of someone who owned the compartment. Bots hung on the back of her hands—gilded and ornate like jewels, the needles on the tips of their bodies almost invisible. As *The Shadow's Child* watched, they withdrew, leaving beads of blood pearling on Long Chau's dark skin.

"Elder aunt—" the bots-handler was looking nervous, and the activity maps were starting to bleed into stress. Useless.

"Come back later, please?" *The Shadow's Child* asked. "I'm sorry, but I have to deal with this."

After her customer was gone, the room reverted to its neutral configuration: not her office with its tasteful decoration of modern paintings of starscapes, and statues of ships and bots. It was now a grey and white space with the polished sheen of metal, and the number and habitat reference of the compartment inscribed on every wall. The only ornaments were her physical bookshelves, crammed full of works Long Chau would no doubt disapprove of.

Long Chau had driven the bots-handler away. Wasted time, a process of mapping The Shadow's Child would have to start from scratch again; wasted money, because the bots' needles would need to be sterilised again. She didn't have money to waste. Or time. "If you want to see me, make an appointment."

"It seemed inefficient. And inappropriate. I'm not here to get a blend. Though I will of course pay you for your time. I wouldn't want to cheat you of your living." A pause, then a look that was no longer nonchalant, but as piercing as a spear's point. "Unless you would deem that offer offensive."

"I don't," *The Shadow's Child* said, less sharply than she'd meant to. Long Chau's payment had been good, but Bao was right: at the rate things were going she'd default on the rent next time it was due. Long Chau seemed to alternate between flashes of singular consideration, and complete disregard of others' feelings. "I don't do misplaced pride."

A pause again; as if Long Chau meant to say something and hadn't. "Fair enough. Anyway, I thought you'd be interested in knowing more as soon as I had it. It's not every day you find a corpse."

Not insofar as she was concerned, for sure. A nudge on *The Shadow's Child*'s implants: an authorisation access limited to sharing data. She hesitated—she didn't like to grant access since she often forgot to revoke it—but accepted. A portrait of a woman—an old-fashioned one in a watercolour style, obviously bots-drawn—the sweeps of colours were too clean, too regular—shimmered on visual. The resemblance was obvious. "Your corpse?"

"Ours. Pham Thi Hai Anh," Long Chau said. "She made a living maintaining the inner rings of the Apricot Blossom Ho habitat."

"I see," *The Shadow's Child* said. She didn't. Curiosity won out, narrowly. "You know what she died of."

"No," Long Chau said. "I'm friends with the controller of deaths: they could find no cause of death. Which means that, having set aside all other possible causes, she was alive and well when she tumbled into deep spaces."

She raised a hand, as if to forestall an objection from *The Shadow's Child*. "The pressures of unreality would have rendered her unconscious within ten divisions, and killed her not long afterwards—a centiday, at most. A shadow skin doesn't protect against deep spaces."

Trying to spare *The Shadow's Child*'s feelings? Or more likely making sure she couldn't be interrupted.

"All right," *The Shadow's Child* said. "So an accident, then."

Long Chau smiled. "I don't know what happened. But I intend to find out."

"I don't understand the urgency."

"The militia is going to take over."

"And? Surely that's good."

"Only if you think the tribunal and the militia competent." Long Chau clearly didn't. Then again, if she'd been involved with them, as a suspect... "They'll take everyone into custody and throw drugs at them in the hopes of finding a ready culprit. By the time they're done, there'll be no evidence or goodwill left to base an investigation on."

Personal experience? She sounded so intense it must have been. But she must also have hated not knowing the answers. "I'm not sure—"

"We have a day, perhaps two," Long Chau said. "At most. The circumstances are unusual, and I've been digging: this will draw their attention faster."

"Look," *The Shadow's Child* said. "I don't know what your relationship with the tribunal is—" though she fully intended to find *that* out—"but I'm not setting myself at odds with them."

Long Chau's glance was puzzled. "Of course not. We'll have solved this long before they intervene, if we move fast enough. That's the point." She stretched, drawing herself to her full height. "I'm going to Apricot Blossom Ho habitat. Care to come?"

"Because you need a ship to take you there?"

Long Chau shrugged. It obviously hadn't even occurred to her. "I can take a shuttle, if you'd rather not."

The Shadow's Child was getting paid, when all was said and done. And she needed the money. And—and she did want to know what had happened—how Hai Anh had died, and if any justice was going to be given to her—even if it was Long Chau's high-handed, arrogant kind.

She could move the two appointments she had in the afternoon, with little harm done. She could go with Long Chau, even for a little while.

"No need," she said. "I'll come."

* * *

In the end, Long Chau did take a shuttle, because traffic was too dense and the Apricot Blossom orbital didn't have a docking bay ready for another bi-hour. *The Shadow's Child* projected her avatar straight into the orbital, and spent some time checking out the new classes of bots for sale in shops. Not that, on her current situation, she could really afford to do more than look and dream.

She'd finally given Long Chau privileged access, which meant Long Chau's calls would be given priority, and that she would also be able to locate her easily. The address Long Chau was headed to wasn't a private compartment, but a wide, airy space with a sign that said "House of Saltless Prosperity".

"Monastery?" *The Shadow's Child* asked, when she arrived.

Long Chau shook her head. "Sisterhood," she said, briefly, using an odd, seldom used word. "Here. You won't be able to materialise straight inside, I'm afraid." It was a map of a maze of linked corridors and compartments, with a single dot at the destination.

"Tell me something," *The Shadow's Child* said.

Long Chau raised an eyebrow.

"The militia took you in for questioning. Why?"

Long Chau didn't move. "You've been digging."

"You did the same thing to me."

Long Chau shook her head. "I deducted based on available information. Not the same."

The Shadow's Child said, stubbornly, "Tell me why."

"See if you can deduce it," Long Chau said, as she headed inside. Her tone made it clear she didn't expect *The Shadow's Child* to manage that.

Her mistake. *The Shadow's Child* would show her.

She followed Long Chau inside. She had the map on sensors and was gliding faster than Long Chau could walk, and yet she was barely able to keep up. The corridors were plain and unadorned, though here and there a painting or a vid broke the monotony. Through half-open doors, she caught a glimpse of faces—women ranging from young to very old, none of them with that particular smoothness of rejuv—their faces taut and thin, not quite at that edge where it'd become starvation. *Sisterhood*, Long Chau had said. That was certainly an unusual place.

When she arrived, Long Chau was seated cross-legged at a low table, already deep in conversation with an old woman. *The Shadow's Child* used the brief interval of time to look up the place on the network. By the time the woman rose, she'd gleaned enough context, but not much.

"This is Grandmother Khue," Long Chau said. "*The Shadow's Child*, who is assisting me."

Grandmother Khue looked as though she'd swallowed something sour, though clearly the ill humour was all directed towards Long Chau. She smiled at *The Shadow's Child*. "I've heard of you," she said.

"I've had contact with your house." *The Shadow's Child* had briefly checked her own records: she'd provided blends for women who lived there—not ones for crossing deep spaces aboard a mindship, but the cheaper, blunter ones, to not feel afraid while teetering on the edge of the vacuum. She'd assigned the rewatch of her interviews with them to her fastest processes on the way there: the only thing that emerged was a vague memory of hunched, tired women who made a point of pride to pay on time.

There was nothing whatsoever hunched, or tired, about Grandmother Khue.

The compartment was small, and the public overlay crammed with things. Unlike in *Sharpening Steel into Needles'* one, it was hard to tell which objects were physical and which ones were not. It looked to be fragments of various wrecks: twisted metal that had taken on the sheen of oil, changed and compressed by deep spaces. The kind of curiosities scholars collected but wouldn't pay much for.

The large, wooden box of a mat chuoc game lay prominently on a commode, open to display the patterns on polished bone tiles. It was an odd, terribly old fashioned choice, but also a casual statement that not everything there was cheap. By its side was a small wooden box carved with the insignia of a brewer of serenity—Nguyen Van An Tam, *The Shadow's Child*'s sensors told her, a minor brewer of the habitat who didn't have much of a reputation or charge much for his services.

It was... not quite genteel poverty, but close.

Grandmother Khue caught her looking. "I salvage in deep spaces. There's always a market for pretty things scholars can display at banquets and poetry club meetings, to impress their friends."

"Not much of a steady job," Long Chau said, coldly.

"Better than being indentured to the families."

Long Chau's face didn't move. "Perhaps."

"You're an odd pair," Grandmother Khue said. "I'm not sure how we can help. Or if we should."

"She was part of your community," Long Chau said.

"She's dead." Grandmother Khue sounded—not like

what *The Shadow's Child* expected. Not grieving, or surprised. Merely angry. Long Chau didn't appear to have picked up on it; or perhaps she merely went on regardless. "We don't want trouble."

"And no justice?" Long Chau's face didn't move. "I could tell the magistrate that. I'm sure they'd find that very interesting."

"If they bother to come at all." Grandmother Khue sat back. "You know exactly how much we mean to the orbitals." There were two cups of tea on the table. She gestured, and a third, ethereal one shimmered into existence for *The Shadow's Child.*

"You keep the belt going," *The Shadow's Child* said, slowly. She floated the tea cup to her; sipped it, feeling a soft, grassy taste—a memory of first meeting *Sharpening Steel into Needles* and the sparks that had flown then; of endless conversations with her family that went on and on into the night, from everything to the examination results of the younger descendants to pregnancies and births and deaths. "You and the other women here." The House of Saltless Prosperity: a loose sisterhood of menials, of women who, like the dead Hai Anh, worked to maintain and clean the orbitals, and who had sworn to be each other's family.

"We're cheap," Grandmother Khue said. "Easily replaceable." She smiled. "Less so if banded together."

"So you do have enemies," Long Chau said.

"The Ho and the other Inner Habitats families?" Grandmother Hue snorted. "You're mistaken."

"Am I?" Long Chau asked.

Grandmother Khue set her tea cup on the table. "I've already asked you why you care."

"I like to solve problems."

"Problem? Hai Anh was a *person*," Grandmother Khue said, sharply.

"I know." Long Chau's face didn't move. "So you do care, but you don't want me to investigate. Interesting." The way she said it, Hai Anh might as well have been a tricky paragraph in some memorial. "Why did she have a shadow skin? It's an expensive investment to make, given a menial's average salary."

"She cleaned the outside of the orbitals," Grandmother Khue said. "And yes, it's expensive, but shadow skins are life insurance. New workers are cheaper than proper suits or climbing pads, so the families don't always bother with proper repairs to equipment. If something they give you fails and you tumble into the vacuum, you'll be glad to have one."

"I see." Long Chau shook her head. "It didn't protect her against deep spaces."

"Nothing does." Grandmother Khue rose, putting her cup of tea on the table. "You can see her compartment. I doubt you'll find anything of use, but—" A younger girl had appeared in the entrance of the room. "Tuyet will show you."

* * *

45

Hai Anh's room was small, and almost bare of life. Not surprising, when all the holos and paintings would have been tied to her, and erased or put offline after her death. Long Chau knelt for a while, staring at the small, cramped bed. A faint smell of sandalwood and incense hung in the air, in front of a statue of Quan Am.

"I missed the beginning of the conversation," *The Shadow's Child* said.

"Not much of use," Long Chau said. "Though I'd be curious how she struck you."

Aggravated by Long Chau, but then again, that was more or less a given. "Competent. A long-time leader. What did she strike you as?"

"'Long-time leader'." Long Chau weighed the words, as if on the tip of her tongue. She didn't like Grandmother Khue—that much was obvious. "Yes. She likes being in control, doesn't she."

"You're the one who reads people."

"Do I?" Long Chau shook her head.

"You seemed to find it easy enough, with me."

"You're a Mind."

"And it's different?"

"Of course it is," Long Chau said.

"Easier?" She didn't usually do that, but something about Long Chau invited challenge. Perhaps the simple knowledge that she'd get an honest answer, even if she didn't like it.

"Different," Long Chau said. "Easier for me, but we both know that's not the case for most people." And then, after a pause that announced a change of subjects, "You have contacts with other shipminds."

"And with other people," *The Shadow's Child* said, sharply.

"You know what I mean," Long Chau said. "I'm not a very social person."

For sure. *The Shadow's Child* bit back the obvious comment. "You want to know why she was in deep spaces."

"Yes. See." Long Chau knelt, bots crawling out of her sleeves. They took, one by one, positions on the bed and at the corners of the low table. Her breathing slowed, for a fraction of a moment. The entire room, walls to floor, was washed with the red of New Year's Eve lanterns—an eye-blink only, and then there were pictures on the walls once more, and a bowl of tangerines on the table, and books by the bed. "That's what she'd have shown to an outside visitor." Long Chau blinked, again, and the books shifted slightly. The bowl of tangerines was joined by papers with broad, thick ink swathes—a suggestion of limbs and claws, of large wings spreading in the vacuum of space. "And to the sisterhood."

"You hacked her room's systems?"

"No," Long Chau said. "I did that when I first came in. I'm just showing you what I've been seeing since."

"All right," *The Shadow's Child* said. "I can ask, but you're aware I don't know every shipmind in the belt." She put out a query to *Sharpening Needles into Steel*, asking them about Hai Anh.

"I need a point of entry, not a personal introduction. All her things still seem to be here—books, vids, tangerines. Nothing in here indicates she was about to leave for a trip of some duration." She knelt, picked up the book on the top shelf. "*Love in the Time of Mulberry Seas*. One of those mythical romances that's been all the rage in the belt." Her tone was dismissive.

"I've read it," *The Shadow's Child* said, sharply. And many of the other titles as well—she and Hai Anh obviously chose books in similar ways.

Long Chau had the grace to relent. "It's well-written. This one is bookmarked." A bot crawled up her hands, settled on her fingertip. "And she'd been making regular progress through it the last few days."

The Shadow's Child's sensors had been trying to flag up something for a while: it finally climbed up the pile of priorities. In the doorway, behind her. She turned and saw the girl who'd accompanied them there—Tuyet?—standing in the narrow doorway, staring open-mouthed at Long Chau.

"You're a medium," she said.

Long Chau's face didn't move. "I don't speak with the spirits. Or the dead. Or only for a very narrow range of definitions of 'speak'."

Not very social. The Shadow's Child bit back a curse, and said, "Was she your friend? Hai Anh?"

Tuyet bit her lip, dancing back and forth. She was young, and thin. She barely looked old enough to have been allowed to join the sisterhood. "She kept to herself, a lot."

"Books and games," Long Chau said, nodding. "She was shy, wasn't she? Not very confident."

"Grandmother Khue said—" Tuyet stopped, and visibly changed what she'd been about to say. "It's a thing that happens to a lot of us. Thinking we're alone and that we don't matter." It sounded like a lecture she herself had been given. "That's why we have the sisterhood."

The Shadow's Child only had a rough idea of what obligations comprised the sisterhood, or of what use Long Chau could possibly think she'd be. *Sharpening Needles into Steel* was, in typical fashion, rounding up all the younger ships and asking about Hai Anh, or sending them to check manifestos. Nothing seemed to stand out: Hai Anh herself never seemed to have been a passenger anywhere. But she had plunged, alive, into deep spaces. There had to be a connection.

"She didn't get on with Grandmother Khue, did she?" Long Chau said.

Tuyet looked startled, but said nothing.

"She locked her communications to the sisterhood, and there was some pretty strong encryption on parts of this room." She made a gesture, and a chessboard appeared on the table, its pieces still scattered in the midst of a game. "It could have been a general quarrel, but nothing else in said communications indicates that. More likely she no longer wanted Grandmother Khue to monitor her."

"She doesn't spy on us!" Tuyet's face was flushed. "You don't understand what it's like. Everyone in the Inner

Habitats families would love to tear us apart. If it means slightly fewer secrets..." She shook her head.

The Shadow's Child bit back a curse. If that was Long Chau's way to solicit witnesses... "The sisterhood were the ones who got you out of trouble."

Tuyet didn't speak. She was watching the chessboard, with an unreadable expression on her face. One bot rested on her wrist, trembling, as if aching to be let loose into the room.

"I've met her kind before," Long Chau said. "She rules. She has to, because disunity is weakness, and the sisterhood can't afford to be weak."

Tuyet was shaking now. "You're making it sound... dirty."

"I proffer no moral judgment." Long Chau picked up one of the chess pieces, looked at it. "A good game, but her opponent was far weaker than her. Did you come here often?"

"Disaster" might be too weak a word for how the interview was turning out. *The Shadow's Child* gave up on all subtlety, and went on the offensive. "You said you'd met Grandmother Khue's kind before. During the uprising?"

Long Chau looked mildly surprised. "I didn't serve, if that's what you're asking for."

The Shadow's Child had, but of course mindships weren't given a choice about whether to enlist. "Can you answer the question?"

Long Chau raised an eyebrow. "I worked for someone

very much like her, once." She looked, again, at Tuyet. Her voice was kinder. "Escaping one cage for another?"

"You don't understand anything," Tuyet said. "She *cares*. My family didn't." Her accent was rough: Outer Habitats, and not the social class that ever saw much of examinations or rising in the world.

A long, uncomfortable silence. At last, Long Chau stretched. "I apologise. I wouldn't want to see you hurt."

"I don't see what makes you think I'd be hurt."

The Shadow's Child was sorting out threads—a low priority one, sending a search query for anyone of Long Chau's age working for an Inner Habitat family; and a higher one, reading through the report *Sharpening the Steel into Needles* had sent through.

In the heartbeat that it took Long Chau to turn towards the table, *The Shadow's Child* read and digested the older shipmind's report. She considered speaking aloud, but then she'd have been no better than Long Chau. Instead, she forwarded her the report, letting Long Chau make her own opinion on it. If nothing else, it would shut her up for a while.

She needed to keep Tuyet busy during that time. A young girl, an infant by shipminds' lives, who looked away from her, who didn't enjoy strangers invading her spaces. Whose prickliness hid a deep unease. Guilt? Not quite that, either—*The Shadow's Child* had seen more than enough guilt in the years of the uprising, more than enough soldiers who'd killed or caused to be killed.

Time for a stab in the dark. "You know how she died, don't you? Or think you do."

No answer.

"*The Sorrow of Four Gentlemen*," *The Shadow's Child* said. "I wasn't aware you had a mindship as a member of the sisterhood."

"He has a past," Long Chau said, unfolding from her trance. "The mindship."

"You read it?" *The Shadow's Child* said. It had been pages and pages of data, none of it in formats friendly for humans. "It was—"

"Long, and hard to digest. I know. I'm fast." Her smile was tight; her movements now fast, with none of that drawn-out languidness, but rather those of a tiger on the trail. "Do you have other questions you want to ask her?"

"I—"

Long Chau unfolded. "We're leaving."

"I don't understand—" Her other search, the one on the Inner Habitat families, was yielding too many results to be of use. Even if she'd known Long Chau's date of birth it would have been useless. Curses.

"I told you before: I don't make guesses," Long Chau said. "But I can read patterns, and I don't like what I'm seeing here."

"You were the one who told me to look up mindships!"

"Yes." Long Chau looked mildly irritated again, as if pausing to explain things to a five-year-old. "Can you trust me for a moment? I know what I'm doing, but I don't have the leisure to explain." She looked, again, at Tuyet. And then, to *The Shadow's Child*'s surprise, she stopped by Tuyet's side, one hand resting lightly on her shoulder. "Be careful, will you? With the mindship."

The girl looked as Long Chau as if she was mad. "He's not a killer." She held herself taut, and behind her was the glimmer of something else—scales and mane and snout, with fine lines showing the gradients of temperature and pressure maintained for her safety and comfort—her own shadow-skin, her life insurance.

"That's not what I said," Long Chau said, shaking her head. She moved away, as if the rest of the conversation was of little import.

The Shadow's Child looked, again, at the small room, the remnants of Hai Anh's life. Tuyet's shadow-skin had vanished back into her clothes, but a hint of its presence remained, darkening the planes of her face. What was Long Chau up to? "I'm coming," *The Shadow's Child* said, finally, though she wasn't sure if that was the right thing to do.

* * *

Outside the House of Saltless Prosperity, *The Shadow's Child* caught up with Long Chau. "Are you ever going to bother explaining?"

Long Chau waved, irritably. "Let's find a teahouse. I don't suppose you do blends outside of deep spaces?"

"You're drugged enough as it is," *The Shadow's Child*

said. How did Long Chau manage to get her angry so quickly?

"Not very much," Long Chau said. "That's part of the issue."

At this hour of the afternoon, the teahouse was deserted, people having left the heart food and tea in favour of dinner in restaurants. Long Chau relaxed back in her chair, her bots clinging to the back of her hands—even without bothering to look, *The Shadow's Child* could see the needles slipping into her skin. By the time the food had arrived on the table, Long Chau was languid once more. The bots didn't vanish. They remained on her hands, their surfaces shining in the teahouse's shifting light.

They were in a private booth. The overlays had been altered by the habitat's Mind to create walls that would muffle most sounds. *The Shadow's Child* had been offered a choice of music, but wanted none: no possible distraction.

"*The Sorrow of Four Gentlemen*," Long Chau said. "Did you ever hear of the Church of Blissful Atonement?"

"No," *The Shadow's Child* said. The words were outsider parlance. "An outsider one?"

"It was outsider-inspired. I doubt whoever set this up really was a believer in their religion." Long Chau hesitated. "They sent their members into deep spaces as part of their services. It kept them humble."

Alone and crushed by unreality—knowing that there were no rules, and that nothing they did or thought would matter, out there—that time was an illusion, death or madness a certainty... Bad for her, considerably worse for humans. *The Shadow's Child* shivered. She sipped at her tea—even if it was merely sensory memory heated up and served to her by the teahouse's network, the taste cleansed her palate. "The mindship."

"Yes. And unreality suits. Mindships, no matter how illusory a protection they might be, stand against deep spaces. Remove that comfort, and you'll have people scared out of their minds and grovelling before you."

She could have looked it up; could have asked the network to tell her what had happened. But she'd have had to look at pictures, at vids, at events. "You used the past tense. I presume something went wrong," she said, slowly. If only her blends worked on herself, and outside of deep spaces.

Long Chau looked at her, for a while. When she started speaking again, her words were slow and measured. Considered. "They left a ten-year-old girl in deep spaces for some time. As a punishment."

"They—" She had no words. At least she was a mindship. At least she could endure it all—even if it wasn't true, even if the thought of diving in deep made her feel cold and squeezed. "The girl—"

"She survived," Long Chau said. "It may not have been a kindness. You'd know this better than I, but the deep spaces altered her brain chemistry." She looked... angry, in a way she hadn't been when she'd seen the corpse—closer to the behaviour she'd had with Tuyet. Was it the age? "It was a long time ago. Shortly after the uprising." She shook her head. "I wasn't consulting, back then, but it made quite a splash."

"I was... not following news," *The Shadow's Child* said. In a dock, being refitted and healed, pored over by an army of doctors and apothecaries, prescribed useless drug after useless drug. Any news like that would have headed the list of things she wasn't allowed to know. "The mindship—"

"*The Sorrow of Four Gentlemen*? Yes," Long Chau said. "The name has changed, of course. He wouldn't be such a fool. He's taking passengers between habitats for a living."

"And you think he's killing people? That's not what you told Tuyet."

"I don't," Long Chau said. "The girl was an accident, and everyone involved was investigated. And jailed, exiled or executed. An unbalanced mindship wouldn't have been allowed to continue carrying people. Or to continue at all." She picked at a translucent shrimp dumpling with her chopsticks, thoughtfully. The bots on her hands shifted, but the needles didn't withdraw. She had to be pumped full by now. Not that it made her any more pleasant.

The Shadow's Child just couldn't muster any pretence of eating.

"He wasn't jailed."

"No," Long Chau said. "And yet here we find him, a decade later, working with a similar organisation."

"There's no common point—"

"You know what I mean. A community of down-trodden people desperate for enlightenment and protection."

"You do them a disservice," *The Shadow's Child* said, mildly. She'd heard that exact rhetoric from Inner Habitat families. In fact... she brought up again her research on Inner Habitat families, and relaunched it, using the expression Long Chau had used.

That was it.

The head of the Golden Carp Tran family had a verbal tic with exactly those words, and a similar accent. *The Shadow's Child* narrowed her search queries again, asking for employment of anyone of Long Chau's approximate age by that particular family and lineage, and correlating it with militia arrests.

"Mmm." Long Chau finished her dumpling, and helped herself to more rice soup. "They're doing the same thing. *The Sorrow of Four Gentlemen* is making regular requests to enter deep spaces. I had a look at a few of the recorded logs: it's always Grandmother Khue, a couple of people from the house, and someone who looks scared."

"That's guesswork, surely," *The Shadow's Child* said, with less bite than she'd meant to. She was distracted by her search, which was showing progress on a high-priority thread. So far, no results. But it was far from done: the list of people who had worked for the family at one time or another was huge.

"No. Analysis of evidence, and converging hypotheses. Call it guesswork if you want. The likelihood of my being right is high enough that I'm confident putting this on the table."

"Still not explaining why Hai Anh would get into deep spaces without an unreality suit."

But the rest of it would fit. It would explain why both Grandmother Khue and Tuyet had felt so guilty. "You think it's a disciplinary matter gone bad?"

"Now *that*," Long Chau said, "would be guesswork. I don't know. There are no recordings for the evening Hai Anh boarded. Someone wiped them, but they weren't thorough enough to go back and wipe every single trip that mindship took into deep spaces." She shook her arms. The bots detached from her hands, and slid back into her sleeves.

"It could also be simple malfunction," *The Shadow's Child* said. "I had a look at the records. *The Sorrow of Four Gentlemen* is in bad shape. The sisterhood doesn't have the money to maintain him. It's a wonder anyone is confident enough to leap into deep spaces with him."

"You're being disingenuous," Long Chau said. "Mindship critical functions and security systems are the last things to go. If he's still able to move and plunge into deep spaces, he wouldn't be able to lose a human life because of a systems failure."

Disingenuous? An easy and hurtful thing to say, as casual as the rest of her comments. "I'm not," *The Shadow's Child* said, slowly. The search was distracting her.

"Hai Anh was caught in strong currents. She could very well have drifted out of sight of the mindship within just a few moments." She forestalled Long Chau's raised hand by speaking faster. "The newer ships would have caught up with her if this happened. But *The Sorrow of Four Gentlemen* is old. Reflexes would be slower."

"I'm going to the docks," Long Chau was saying. "That ship takes regular trips with passengers, which means he'll be around one way or another. I want to have a look at him."

"Mmm." The search was ending: only one result. She opened the related files; stared as she processed.

Long Chau said, "If there's any regularity, their next trip into deep spaces should be quite soon."

The Shadow's Child listened distractedly, because of the file. She'd intended to process its contents quietly and have a chance to confront Long Chau after due deliberation, but what she saw—

"Kim Oanh," *The Shadow's Child* said.

Long Chau had been about to rise from the table. She sat down now. The languidness was gone, leaving only the sharp, fast and wounding edge of a blade. "What did you say?"

"Tran Thi Kim Oanh," *The Shadow's Child* said, slowly, deliberately. "You were her teacher, weren't you?" Long Chau had changed her appearance. Not a very deep or a particularly careful job, but it didn't need to be, not when the uprising had upended so many things in the Scattered Pearls belt—and of course seven years would change a person, regardless.

"That's none of your business."

"I think," *The Shadow's Child* said, slowly, "that I'd want to know what happened, before letting you loose into the company of girls like Tuyet."

Long Chau stared, and said nothing.

A sixteen-year-old girl, chafing at the strictures of family life—vanished without a trace, with dark speculations she'd simply been sold into slavery, or to a bidder with tastes for a young and pliant concubine. An entire household, relatives and servants taken into the tribunal for interrogation—nothing of any significance turning up, just a girl that remained missing, seven years down the line, and everyone knowing what this really meant.

Long Chau's hands were shaking. The bots came out again. They hovered on her wrists, but didn't inject anything. She spoke at last, saying, simply, "The tribunal questioned me. Extensively. I'm still here. Not jailed or exiled or executed."

"Like *The Sorrow of Four Gentlemen*?" *The Shadow's Child* said.

"Touché."

"Talk to me."

"Why should I?"

"Because you got me to come along. Because the least you owe me is the truth." Because she'd split open *The Shadow's Child* like a pomegranate, leaning on old wounds until they bled red and ripe—dissecting her like the corpse in the hangar bay, and then walking away when the problem was no longer of interest.

"Do I?" Long Chau watched her, for a while. *The Shadow's Child* didn't move—cycling between pictures of her pitted hull, of the dark and blackened shape of her motors—of the painting of the Azure Dragons gardens on the front, the one Mother and her long-dead sister had carefully etched.

At length, Long Chau rose from the table. Her hands were still again, her movements slow and careful. There was none of that cooped energy about her now, simply anger. "You're mistaken. I don't have to talk to you. I told you before: deductions, not guesses."

"I'm not you!"

"Patently not. Now if you'll excuse me—"

"You're just going to walk away?"

Long Chau didn't even bother to turn.

"I'll tell them," *The Shadow's Child* said. "The house." And then she stopped, for why would they trust her more than they did Long Chau?

"Feel free," Long Chau said. And she walked out, without looking back.

* * *

When she got back to her office, the lights were still on, and the remnants of the abortive interview with her previous customer were still on. The bots scattered across the floor, picking themselves up when she entered, the activity map automatically opening up for her to check.

She didn't feel like any of that.

A sixteen-year-old girl.

She'd thought Long Chau was prickly and uncaring, but *that* was something else.

Control, *Sharpening Steel into Needles* had said. A currency you've always been short of.

Currently, she had so little she could have laughed. Or wept, or both.

In the end, she did the only thing she could think of, though it was neither pleasant nor relaxing: she called Bao.

Bao took the call almost immediately. She was in her office, in the midst of immaculate bookshelves with carefully aligned books, all matching editions, battered and creased. "Ship?" Wary surprise.

The Shadow's Child said, carefully, "It's not about the rent." It was, in a way—because Long Chau was no longer going to be paying her, because she'd wasted all that time on an investigation she couldn't trust when she should have been taking care of her pitifully few customers—but she couldn't tell Bao that. Not now.

"Oh?"

"I need some information," *The Shadow's Child* said. "On an Inner Habitat family." She saw Bao shift, and said, "Not the Western Pavilion Le."

Bao relaxed a fraction. No conflicting loyalties, then. The book on her desk was physical: yellowed with age, stained with brown like an old man's skin. It looked like one of the cheap editions of an early Lao Quy, *The Jade and the Deer,* something that didn't actually have that much value except sentimental. "Why not. Ask."

"Tran Thi Kim Oanh," *The Shadow's Child* said.

"The Golden Carp Tran." Bao watched her, carefully. Her bots moved, like the swaying branches of a willow tree. "That's old history. What's the interest?"

"It came up," *The Shadow's Child* said.

Bao raised an eyebrow. "Really."

She—she was going to have to give something, or she'd get nothing. "The teacher. I think—" Far, far away in her heartroom, she tasted bile. "I think she's one of my customers."

She'd thought Bao was going to mock her about morality, but instead the woman's face went still: a truly unsettling effect, because it'd had very little expression to start with. "It was a sordid affair," she said, finally. "It made a big impression in high society when it happened. Kim Oanh was sixteen and rather sheltered. You know how those things go. She wanted more of life; her family wanted to keep her safe, and to ensure the best future for her."

"And her teacher?"

"The teacher was arrogant."

What a surprise. "Trouble with the family?"

"She'd gone past some lines, yes. Following her own ideas and reproving the elders as if she weren't a subordinate years their junior."

Typical Long Chau—seven years ago, and not so different. "I'm surprised they kept her on."

"The eldest grandmother liked her. There were... many

arguments on the proper behaviour, which slowed things down. And before they could dismiss her—"

"Kim Oanh vanished."

"Yes. It was the birthday of the family's eldest grandmother, and everyone had gone to pay their respects. Kim Oanh was sick and it looked contagious, so she was meant to attend through the network, with the teacher keeping an eye on her. When she didn't come on, they came back in a panic. She was gone, and the teacher professed not to have noticed anything."

An obvious suspect. "I assume the militia looked."

"They did more than look," Bao said. "Nothing conclusive came up, but—" she hesitated.

"Go on," *The Shadow's Child* said. It could hardly get worse.

"Several months after the investigation closed, your teacher came into possession of rather too much money. It was traced back to people smugglers."

"Slavers." She kept her voice flat, emotionless. She had to, or she'd burst.

"I don't know," Bao said. "The tribunal didn't find any conclusive evidence it was tied to Kim Oanh."

"The family would have pressed," *The Shadow's Child* said. Surely many rules could bend and break, when money and influence were involved?

"They did," Bao said. "The magistrate is a stickler for rules, and they didn't appreciate their hand being forced in that clumsy a manner. So it stopped there."

Seven years ago. A year before the uprising that tore

the belt apart. So easy for a wayward, suspect teacher to slip away, and to reinvent herself as a dilettante detective—to take on cases to amuse herself, living on blood money.

In fact—

Long Chau still had the money. In all likelihood, she'd used it to pay *The Shadow's Child*.

The Shadow's Child was going to be sick.

"You've gone very silent," Bao said. "She paid you, didn't she? That big lump transaction you gave me access to the other day—"

Too sharp, but then Bao hadn't gotten to where she was by being stupid.

"I'll sort things out," *The Shadow's Child* said, slowly, carefully. She felt, dimly, her core stretch against the connectors in the heartroom, their reassuring coolness against her.

She'd return it. She'd find some other way to earn her living—more customers, or perhaps some deliveries on the edge of deep spaces. Something. Anything.

"I see," Bao said. And then, with a shake of her head, "You worry too much about morality."

"Don't you?" *The Shadow's Child* said.

"The tribunal thought she was innocent."

"Not innocent. Just not guilty. That's not the same." Words seemed to have turned to tar—to come, slowly and inexorably, from her physical body, shivering in the heartroom.

"I don't judge," Bao said.

"You offered me the office space. To a shipmind."

"Precisely. You could pay. That was a calculated risk. I didn't pass moral judgments on what you were or weren't."

"I—"

"For what it's worth, I'd say in your current position, you can ill afford to pick and choose on mere suspicions." Bao rose, and picked a book from the shelves—an electronic. She held it towards *The Shadow's Child*, cover turned up to reveal the flowing calligraphy of a Lao Quy title, with the sharply coloured characters against the background of stars and ships. "You look like you could use a distraction. Here. You've probably read it cover to cover ten thousand times, but it's still good."

After she cut off the connection, *The Shadow's Child* remained in her office, staring at the bookshelves.

They deemed her innocent.

No. They'd merely thought there wasn't enough evidence to declare her guilty. It was a different set of standards—one to weigh a possible execution against.

Mere suspicions, Bao had said.

But what if it were true? The evidence was just too compelling to be ignored; and Long Chau stubbornly refused to offer any explanation or any justification for what had happened.

As if she didn't have any defence.

The Shadow's Child tried to go back to her blends— to the bots-handler and the activity maps she needed to build, the blend she'd have to carefully build—something that would make the handler feel subtly more assured, less fearful—but everything kept sliding off, and she couldn't seem to focus on anything.

Sharpening Steel into Needles pinged her, once, twice. There was some sort of celebration with other ship-minds: an official event with Official Truc, an exiled scholar of the third rank who was going to regale them with his own poems in the presence of most of the high society of the orbitals. *Sharpening Steel into Needles* was going both to enjoy themselves, and to push forward some of the younger ships in the hopes of getting them positions with officials or families. They wanted *The Shadow's Child* to go, of course. It would do her good to get out.

The Shadow's Child didn't want to get out. And the last thing she wanted was *Sharpening Steel into Needles* dragging her around. Her response was terse, and obviously sharp enough that the older ship didn't even insist.

She climbed back into her own body—curled up in her heartroom, withdrawing from her sensors and letting go of her bots, space stretching around her, vast and cold and unchanging, the wind whispering against her hull like a lullaby—the sharp light of the stars a restful, familiar sight. It was the busy time of day, with many ordinary ships ferrying everything from people to crates of food from habitat to habitat, their coms chatter a soothing presence in the background.

She settled down to watch a vid of *The Turtle and the Sword*: familiar characters from empress to concubines, caught in soothing, distant drama—questions of who was the real mother of the prince, and whether the disgraced general would ever get their revenge...

Something was blinking, in her notifications. Long Chau. She didn't want to hear from Long Chau. It was going to be another high-handed request for help, or company, with explanations doled out only when it suited her.

But it wasn't from her.

The sender was a Tran Thi Cam, a controller of deaths working at the tribunal—shared with both her and Long Chau, with a few layers of obfuscations to make it seem anonymous. Amateur work, and nothing that stood up to *The Shadow's Child*'s first few probes.

It was an autopsy report on the corpse they'd found. Why in Heaven had Long Chau or Tran Thi Cam thought this would be relevant? She was about to close it when a line caught her eye.

"Decomposition was, in effect, halted by deep spaces, enabling the recovery of trace amounts of the following."

The list of compounds that followed was extensive: crushed honeydreamer, ginseng, winged sai seeds, and a host of other familiar things.

A blend. That wouldn't have been a cause for concern—blends were common—but the ingredients list was odd, considering everything they'd known about Hai Anh.

Her coms blinked again. This time, it was Long Chau. She sent back a message that she wasn't interested, and of course Long Chau kept calling. She dropped it to a lower priority routine, and tried to focus again.

No use. A centiday later, she'd read just one line of the report, and thought of nothing but the steady blink of that call.

She took it.

"I'm not interested," she said. And then saw the location from which the call was made.

Long Chau's voice was cool. "You should be."

"You're in deep spaces?"

"In a frozen ship." A trace of amusement. Her voice was off, but *The Shadow's Child* wasn't sure why. "You were right. Maintenance on *The Sorrow of Four Gentlemen* was really shoddy."

"You stole aboard—No one steals aboard mindships!"

"The old ones, with blind spots all over their corridors? Easy."

"You—" And then professional instinct took over. "You told me you couldn't function in deep spaces."

"I stole a blend," Long Chau said. "From the kitchen stores. Looks like the sisterhood is keeping it in reserve to help its inductees remain sane in deep spaces. I have to grant them this: they have no intention of breaking anyone past repair." The admission sounded like it cost her.

Too many things, too many problems. Alarms were going off at every level of *The Shadow's Child*'s processes. And she still didn't know if she could trust Long Chau. "They're feeding the same blend to different people? You can't do that. Blends are tailored to one person."

"I didn't think you could."

"You drank one," *The Shadow's Child* pointed out.

"Not much choice."

Why was she surprised Long Chau would get herself into trouble, and fast? And the voice...

She knew exactly what was wrong with the voice. "You're drunk."

"I think not."

Not quite, but it was the fastest way *The Shadow's Child* could explain that Long Chau's thought processes were currently warped by a blend not meant for her. "Is Tuyet onboard?"

"She and Grandmother Khue and a host of other folks I don't know. I'm not sure I get your sense of urgency."

"Then why are you calling me?"

"So you can rescue me, of course. Coms look to be down as well. They're putting a backup transmitter together, but I'll have lost patience long before any rescuing does happen. Not to mention functionality."

Blends. A delicate balance of compounds fed to one person, monitored to be sure they had no adverse effects. Expensive, of course, and the sisterhood was tight for money. They'd pay someone not very much. Someone like Nguyen Van An Tam, the brewer who gave Grandmother Khue her cheap blends. And they'd get a shoddily made job, and...

Breathe. In a room at the heart of her was her core— her self, plugged into connectors and then into the ship, hanging in the vastness of space, and nothing could touch her there.

An easy way to deal with folks like Grandmother Khue

and Long Chau was simply to crank the self-confidence as high as it would go. It worked, though it wasn't subtle. But with folks like Hai Anh—mousy and quiet, fighting with low sense of worth, unaccustomed to trusting themselves—blends like these made them reckless. Terminally drunk.

How did a mindship let someone out into deep spaces? If the person—Hai Anh—themselves did it. If in the airlock, instead of putting on the unreality suit as anyone functional would, they stepped outside, so intoxicated they thought their shadow skin would protect them.

Tuyet.

Tuyet was young, and scarred; and with the same kind of tricky profile as Hai Anh. Not someone whose self-esteem could be so casually boosted.

Not without consequences.

"*Shadow's Child*? Ship?" Long Chau's voice, barely tinged with concern. "What's happening with Tuyet?"

She still didn't know what Long Chau wanted with Tuyet, or what had happened seven years ago. But—

There were two people, currently, who could help Tuyet: her and Long Chau.

And she was too far away. She'd just put in a request for a mindship to rescue *The Sorrow of Four Gentlemen*, who now hung in deep spaces—not on the edges, where she'd taken Long Chau, but deep inside, where Hanh and Vinh and her crew had died, where time stretched to an eternity with no meaning, and space curved back onto itself—he was wounded and broken, just as she'd once been—but

71

no, she couldn't afford to think of that—she needed to focus on what was happening. Too many ships around the orbitals, and Traffic Harmony was unresponsive.

It was Long Chau or no one. "I'm getting help," she said, sharply. "Just keep an eye on Tuyet."

No answer, but then why had she expected one?

Traffic Harmony suddenly came online. "I'm not sure I see the need," they said in an emotionless voice. "It's not an emergency. The mindship's critical functions are still working."

"Someone—" *The Shadow's Child* tried to sort out her thoughts, to convey more information than the fragmented panic she felt. "Someone is going to die."

"I don't understand. Surely, if a mindship is needed, you could go?"

The thought of diving into deep spaces, of losing herself, all over again— "Can you just find another mindship? Any mindship? Someone who can come and help them?"

Long Chau's cool voice in her ears, taking priority over the com with Traffic Harmony. "I'm afraid we have a problem."

"We what—?"

A silence, accompanied by an odd rush. "Can you see where I am? Exactly?"

"Yes, but—"

"Good," Long Chau said. "You have a centiday. Perhaps a little more, but I wouldn't count on it. And now if you'll excuse me, I'll need all my concentration."

"What—?"

"You're smart: you can most probably make the necessary deductions."

She'd expected the call to cut, but it didn't. What happened was that Long Chau fell silent, and she heard a familiar rush of air: a mindship's airlock, dilating open, and then profound silence, only Long Chau's breath, coming slow and measured.

A centiday. The time it would take for a human being in deep spaces to start dying.

"Please tell me you have an unreality suit," she said to Long Chau. If Tuyet didn't have it...

She could almost hear Long Chau say she wasn't a fool—but again, there was no answer.

Long Chau had turned on the suit's sensors. That was now the only thing *The Shadow's Child* was getting from her: a body, tumbling away, and a shadow skin torn to shreds by the pressures of unreality, all of it growing larger and larger as Long Chau propelled herself to catch Tuyet. Tuyet's eyes were closed, her face swollen—her skin flushed the colour of bruises, changing and shifting in successive washes of alien colours.

A centiday.

If she stopped—if she thought, truly, really, about what she was going to do—she would freeze.

"Traffic Harmony?"

"Yes?"

"I need to enter deep spaces."

A heartbeat—a slow, agonising one—before the

authorisation came through, tinged with more than a hint of puzzlement.

She took in a deep breath, and dived in.

It was restful at first. Oily light crept along her hull, things shifting and changing, a cavernous noise like the booming of a heartbeat, resonating in her corridors, being held and loved—and then, as she got deeper in, as the light changed—as the cold seared the metal of her hull, as the warmth turned into a spike that seemed to pierce her heartroom and her core, she remembered.

Corpses. Lieutenant Hanh, torn apart as the rebel ship took out the docking bay, her sharp and angular face above the ruin of her body. The damage spreading out, engulfing the living quarters and the motors and driving through her entire body, incinerating paintings and furniture on its way to the heartroom. The privates, scattered in her now airless corridors, their screams and moans as they died still resonating in her memories. And Captain Vinh, struggling to reach the heartroom, her face tightening and changing, her skin awash in light—deep spaces pulling her apart and the scrabbling on the heartroom's door giving way to a low whimper, and then nothing. *The Shadow's Child* reaching, again and again, for controls that slid out of her grasps, feeling everything grow distant and meaningless, her bots clattering one after the other, her corridors growing numb, until only the cold and empty heartroom remained, locked tight, as if any locks and double doors could change anything going on outside...

Turn back.

There was still time. She had to—

"I can't," she whispered.

Long Chau had reached Tuyet. She'd wrapped her arms around the girl. She was fumbling, trying to shield the girl from deep spaces. As if she could: there was no protection there, not from what was shredding the shadow skin to unrecognisable filaments, and turning the body the colour and harshness of jade. Long Chau turned, for a moment. The link showed the dark, faraway shape of *The Sorrow of Four Gentlemen*. She said, slowly, "Tran Thi Kim Oanh."

It was such an incongruous thing that *The Shadow's Child* forgot, for a moment, where she was.

"She was my student," Long Chau said. "A bright, quick girl—a delight to teach." Again, no emotion. No hint of where she was, of what she was recollecting. "Such an intellect. If she'd been allowed to be properly trained—"

They were tumbling deeper and deeper, carried away by the current, everything blurring and shifting around them. Tuyet's face rested on Long Chau's shoulder, her long hair turning dark and brittle, breaking away in chunks—her tears turning into hard, jeweled things—eyes starting to bulge out. "Until she vanished," *The Shadow's Child* said. She was surprised to find old, familiar anger, strong enough to burn away everything else. "On your watch."

A silence. Then. "Her family wanted her to enter the army," Long Chau said. "The fastest way for her to rise—to earn honour and reputation for the family. It was a disappointing choice. A waste of my work and of my time."

"A waste?" She was now so angry she shook. In the background, her motors continued to run, fuelling the dive, the minute adjustments that made her leap from point to point, struggling to hold her course against the currents of unreality. "That's why you decided to earn your money the other way."

"You don't understand." Long Chau's voice was mild. "She asked me to help her vanish. I had to choose which loyalty to uphold—to her, or to her family. Not that it was much of a choice, in the end. The answer was obvious."

"She—"

"She's alive and well. I get messages, sometimes." *The Shadow's Child* couldn't see the smile, but she could imagine it all too well—slow and lazy and gradually taking over Long Chau's entire face. "And if the price for that is people wondering about what I did—let them wonder. The tribunal did interrogate me, but there are ways to mislead them, if you're determined enough."

"The money—"

"She paid me. For, ah. Services rendered."

"You—you let her family think that she was dead." *The Shadow's Child* was almost there. The pressure against her hull was now unbearable. Claws, raking her again and again, a memory of struggling, powerless and broken, hearing only the screams of the dying.

She—

She could do this.

"Of course. The moment they find out she's not, they'll hunt her down and drag her back home. For her own good." The sarcasm in her voice was almost unbearable.

And Tuyet—of course Tuyet, young and running away from family troubles, would remind Long Chau of her former student.

"Your time is almost up," Long Chau said, sharply. In her arms, Tuyet hung limp. Her fingers bent at odd angles, and black hard beads streamed from her nails and hair. "Tell me that was useful."

She could *see* them now, not at a remove through the suit's coms feed, but through her own sensors. Two bodies—Long Chau's tall and bulky shape holding Tuyet tight, arms and legs wrapped around the other woman's hardening, fragmenting body.

One last jump—into the darkness where she'd once so desperately prayed for an end, through space that felt dark and heavy, like hands desperately trying to drag her down one last time. And then she was close enough to both of them to touch, to open an airlock and send bots and a shuttle to retrieve them.

"I'm here," she said.

* * *

The militia was not happy. They knew Long Chau, but they certainly didn't expect to be called from a hospital and handed a case that was almost shut. But they took it in stride, with visible ill grace.

After they were out of hospital—after Long Chau had watched, silent and composed, as Tuyet came out, sleeping on sweat-drenched sheets, with thin, round scars on the tips of her fingers, and a skin the unhealthy colour of funeral shrouds—Long Chau headed straight for the tribunal and the holding cells.

Much to *The Shadow's Child*'s surprise, the militia let them both in.

Grandmother Khue was waiting for them there, seated on the hard floor of the cell, under the soft, unforgiving light from above. She looked pale and exhausted, eyes bruised, nothing of her earlier self-confidence.

"She'll live," Long Chau said. She was leaning against the wall, the bots clinging to her hands again. Only *The Shadow's Child*, who'd insisted on monitoring her and who now had several bots nesting on Long Chau's body, knew how close to sheer exhaustion she was running. "Through no fault of yours."

Grandmother Khue said nothing.

The Shadow's Child said, slowly, "I'd guess it would be negligence rather than murder." They weren't going to charge the brewer, of course—just like an apothecary wouldn't be held responsible if the dosages prescribed weren't respected. It was all on the sisterhood's shoulders.

Long Chau said nothing. She didn't need to. She positively radiated anger—the same carefully set expression she'd had when they'd carried Tuyet into hospital—when she'd sat, tightly focused, until the doctors came out with their verdict—everything not all right, of course, because things never were that simple—but at least offering a measure of hope.

"You had to know," *The Shadow's Child* said. She couldn't help it. She was trying to be kind—to not be Long Chau—but it was hard. "Blends just can't—"

"There were other alerts." Long Chau didn't move from the wall. "Near misses. You're lucky it didn't happen before." Her tone was unbearably light.

Grandmother Khue said, at last—and it looked as though every word was costing her—"I didn't know. I thought—deep spaces are frightening. It was supposed to make things easier."

"To control your flock."

"You don't understand." Again, that visible effort to speak up, as if the air had turned to metal in her mouth. "The Church used it to make people insignificant, but that's not—" she paused, started again. "When you're out there, with no one and nothing to stand in your way—when you realise how small you are—you also realise that everything that ever was, that ever will be, is connected to you. That we're all, in the end, part of the same great thing."

The stuff of nightmares, and she wanted to make it into some kind of revelation? "Buddhist nonsense," *The Shadow's Child* said, sharply.

She'd expected Long Chau to say something, but Long Chau was oddly silent. Reminiscing, the bots said.

"For the right person, perhaps," Long Chau said, at last. She shook her head. "Neither Tuyet nor Hai Anh were, I fancy."

"They would have been. They just had to let go of fear."

Long Chau sighed. She turned, halfway, to look at *The Shadow's Child*. "Always easier to say than do. And it shouldn't take deaths for you to learn that lesson."

"I did what I had to."

"It's pointless," *The Shadow's Child* said to Long Chau, more kindly than she'd meant to. In truth, she was as shaken and as exhausted as Long Chau, and if she even so much as attempted to rest she'd see, again and again, the two bodies tumbling away from her in deep spaces, and feel herself, in the split moment before she finally dived, so close to failing them both. "Come on."

And—much to her surprise—Long Chau did.

* * *

Long Chau walked *The Shadow's Child* back to her office, in silence. Inside, she pulled up a chair, and didn't so much sit as collapse into it. *The Shadow's Child*, unsure of where any of it left them, let the bots prepare tea and dumplings on an almost automatic course.

The room was bare again. She forced herself to turn it into a living space: to make paintings and vids emerge out of the metal space, tweaking them to show stars, and the waterfalls on some distant planet. No deep spaces, though perhaps one day she'd be able to bear this particular sight so close to her. Bookshelves shimmered into existence on the overlay—crammed with mythical romances and sweeping, epic novels of scholars and ships; with heavy tomes on blend-making from basics to more complex subjects. She ached to be alone again, except that silence scared her more than she could say.

Long Chau sat, watching her tea as if it held the secrets of the universe. On her hands, the bots glinted. Probably only the drugs kept her upright. It'd have been a time for apologies, except *The Shadow's Child* didn't feel she owed any.

"What now?" she asked, instead.

Long Chau smiled, a ghost of her earlier expression. "I would go look for another corpse for my memoir, but I don't feel like I could handle the consequences just right now."

"The blend—"

"It's out of my system." She'd refused to let the doctors look at her. Of course. "And I'll be out of your life, soon, never fear. All debts paid."

Her rent. She ought to have felt relieved, but she had no energy for anything. "I see." A pause, then, "You needn't worry. About my telling Kim Oanh's family."

A raised eyebrow. "I hadn't thought you would."

"You didn't have to tell me."

"You dived into deep spaces to rescue Tuyet and me. I know exactly how much that cost you. The least I could do was repay that trust."

"I didn't do it for you."

"I know you didn't. That doesn't change anything." Long Chau was silent, again. She shook her hands: the bots withdrew, leaving only dark, scarred skin beneath them, with barely a drop of blood.

"If you trust me—"

"Yes?"

"Tell me about the drugs. The ones you're taking."

"Oh." Long Chau set the cup on the table. "Not much to tell, is there. You still think it's because of the militia interrogation?" A shadow of her old amusement. "It would be neat, wouldn't it? An easy and sympathetic explanation. Well, I'm sorry to disappoint. I simply need the drugs to function. That's all there is to it. Life isn't easy and neat."

"You make it sound like it is. When you make your deductions from the smallest scraps of evidence."

"When I deduce things? You're mistaken. The world is chaotic and without sense. But in the smallest of spheres it's sometimes possible to straighten things out; to make it seem as though everything means something." She sipped the tea. So did *The Shadow's Child*, letting the memories of family and warmth fill her thoughts. A comfort, though a scant one.

"You sound like Grandmother Khue." She felt only a fraction of her old anger. "Looking for meaning in deep spaces."

Long Chau shook her head. "Still angry?"

"There's nothing out there," *The Shadow's Child* said.

"No revelations. Nothing to worship." But nothing to fear, either.

"Mmm," Long Chau said. What had it been like for her—in those long moments when she was there, desperately trying to hold on to Tuyet and praying to her ancestors—or whoever else she did pray to—that *The Shadow's Child* was going to reach her in time? "As I said—I don't speculate." A pause, then: "But I'm not like Grandmother Khue. I don't endanger young girls. Or ships."

"I know," *The Shadow's Child* said, finally. Long Chau meant well. She was abrasive and forthright, and prone to getting carried away with her own deductions, missing all the subtle cues that would have told anyone else to stop. She—

She was all right, really. "You can come back. When you need a blend. I'll be quite happy to help you. Honestly."

Long Chau set the cup on the table. "Thank you." She rose. Barely the faintest of tremors in her legs, as *The Shadow Child*'s bots left her hair and hands and scuttled onto the floor.

At the door, she stopped, looking in. She thought for a while, and then said, carefully, "If—I should happen to have a case where a shipmind's perspective would be useful—"

"Go on," *The Shadow's Child* said, unsure of what else to say.

Long Chau's gaze was piercing. "I would offer to pay you, but that would be insulting to you and what you do.

So why don't I come to see you, as a friend, and you can tell me what help you'd feel comfortable giving me, and on what terms?"

As a friend. "I'll be glad to," *The Shadow's Child* said—and was surprised to find that she meant it.

Acknowledgements

This book was written at a particularly challenging time in my life, when I was learning to conciliate motherhood of two small children, work and writing. I would like to thank a number of people for the support they provided, without which I would never have made it to the end: Alis Rasmussen, Zen Cho, Vida Cruz, Tade Thompson, Fran Wilde, Michelle Sagara, Stephanie Burgis, Victor Fernando R. Ocampo, Patricia Mulles, Cindy Pon, Nene Ormes, Likhain, Rochita Loenen-Ruiz, Inksea, Alessa Hinlo, D Franklin, Zoe Johnson, Liz Bourke, Mary Robinette Kowal, Elizabeth Bear and Scott Lynch.

Thanks as well to Ava Jarvis, Lynn E. O'Connacht, Seth Gorden, Samantha Henderson, and Genevieve Cogman for providing feedback on the drafts of this, and to Jonathan L. Howard for his speedy reading and blurbing! And to Patrick Samphire and Sebb for advice on covers and lettering.

To everyone who turned this from a draft into a gorgeous book: Yanni Kuznia, Geralyn Lance and everyone at Subterranean Press; Maurizio Manzieri and Dirk Berger for gorgeous and striking cover art; Lisa Rodgers, Patrick Disselhorst and everyone at JABberwocky who worked on this; and my agent John Berlyne for his support and advice.

To my readers and tireless promoters: I wouldn't be here without you.

To Jeremy Brett and Lucy Liu, the Sherlock Holmes and Doctor Watson of my heart.

And, finally, to my parents, who gave 10-year-old me a much coveted two-volume edition of all the Sherlock Holmes stories; to my sister, who geeked with me on Victorian London, TV series and movies; to my husband Matthieu and his wild fixes to plot problems; and to my children, the snakelet and the librarian, who will one day hear about space detectives and their adventures!

Read on for an excerpt of
The Citadel of Weeping Pearls,
a short novel also set in the
Xuya Universe...

The Officer

There was a sound, on the edge of sleep: Suu Nuoc wasn't sure if it was a bell and a drum calling for enlightenment; or the tactics-master sounding the call to arms; in that breathless instant—hanging like a bead of blood from a sword's blade—that marked the boundary between the stylised life of the court and the confused, lawless fury of the battlefield.

"Book of Heaven, Book of Heaven."

The soft, reedy voice echoed under the dome of the ceiling; but the room itself had changed—receding, taking on the shape of the mindship—curved metal corridors with scrolling columns of memorial excerpts, the oily sheen of the Mind's presence spread over the watercolours of starscapes and the carved longevity character at the head of the bed—for a confused, terrible moment as Suu Nuoc woke up, he wasn't sure if he was still in his bedroom in the Purple Forbidden City on the First Planet, or hanging, weightless, in the void of space.

It wasn't a dream. It was the mindship: *The Turtle's*

Golden Claw, the only one addressing Suu Nuoc with that peculiar form of his title, the one that the Empress had conferred on him half out of awe, half out of jest.

The Turtle's Golden Claw wasn't there in his bedroom, of course: she was a Mind, an artificial intelligence encased in the heartroom of a ship; and she was too heavy to leave orbit. But she was good at things; and one of them was hacking his comms, and using the communal network to project new surroundings over his bedroom.

"Ship," he whispered, the words tasting like grit on his tongue. His eyes felt glued together; his brain still fogged by sleep. "It's the Bi-Hour of the Tiger." People plotted or made love or slept the sleep of the just; they didn't wake up and found themselves dragged into an impossible conversation.

But then, of course, *The Turtle's Golden Claw* was technically part of the Imperial family: before her implantation in the ship that would become her body, the Mind had been borne by Thousand-Heart Ngoc Ha, the Empress's youngest daughter. *The Turtle's Golden Claw* was mostly sweet; but sometimes she could act with the same casual arrogance as the Empress.

"What is it this time?" Suu Nuoc asked.

The Turtle's Golden Claw's voice was thin and quivering; nothing like her usual, effortless arrogance. "She's not answering. I called her again and again, but she's not answering."

Ten thousand words bloomed into Suu Nuoc's mind;

were sorted out as ruthlessly as he'd once sorted out battalions. "Who?" he said.

"Grandmother."

There were two people whom the mindship thought of as Grandmother; but if the Keeper of the Peace Empress had been dead, Suu Nuoc's quarters would have been in effervescence, the night servants barely containing their impatience at their master's lack of knowledge. "The Grand Master of Design Harmony?"

The lights flickered around him; the characters oozed like squeezed wounds. "She's not answering," the ship said, again; sounding more and more like the child she was with every passing moment. "She was here; and then she... faded away on the comms."

Suu Nuoc put out a command for the system to get in touch with Grand Master of Design Harmony Bach Cuc—wondering if that would work, with the shipmind hacked into his comms. But no; the progress of the call appeared overlaid on the bottom half of his field of vision, same as normal; except, of course, that no one picked up. Bach Cuc's last known location, according to the communal network, was in her laboratory near the Spire of Literary Eminence—where the radio comms towards *The Turtle's Golden Claw* would be clearest and most economical.

"Did you hack the rest of my comms?" he asked—even as he got up, pulling up clothes from his autumn chest, unfolding and discarding uniforms that seemed too formal; until he found his python tunic.

"You know I didn't." *The Turtle's Golden* Claw's voice was stiff.

"Had to ask," Suu Nuoc said. He pulled the tunic over his shoulders, stared at himself in the mirror by the four seasons chests: pale and dishevelled, his hair hastily pulled back into a topknot—but the tunic was embroidered with pythons, a mark of the Empress's special favour, bestowed on him after the battle at Four Stations: a clear message, for those who affected not to know who he was, that this jumped-up, uncouth soldier wielded authority by special dispensation.

The call was still ringing in the emptiness; he cut it with a wave of his hands. There was a clear, present problem; and in such situations he knew exactly what to do.

"Let's go," he said.

* * *

Grand Master Bach Cuc's laboratory was spread around a courtyard: at this late hour, only the ambient lights were on, throwing shadows on the pavement—bringing to mind the old colonist superstitions of fox shapeshifters and blood-sucking demons.

It was the dry season in the Forbidden Purple City, and Bach Cuc had set up installations on trestle tables in the courtyard—Suu Nuoc didn't remember what half the assemblages of wires and metal were, and didn't much care.

"Where was she when you saw her last?" he asked *The Turtle's Golden Claw.*

The ship couldn't descend from orbit around the First Planet, of course; she'd simply animated an avatar of herself. Most mindships chose something the size of a child or a Mind; *The Turtle's Golden* Claw's avatar was as small as a clenched fist, but perfect, rendering in exquisite detail the contours of her hull, the protrusions of her thrusters—if Suu Nuoc had been inclined to squint, he was sure he'd have caught a glimpse of the orchids painted near the prow.

"Inside," *The Turtle's Golden Claw* said. "Tinkering with things." She sounded like she'd recovered; her voice was cool again, effortlessly taking on the accents and vocabulary of the court. She made Suu Nuoc feel like a fish out of water; but at least he wouldn't have to deal with a panicked, bewildered mindship—he was no mother, no master of wind and water, and would have had no idea how to do in this situation.

He followed the ship into one of the largest pavilions: the outside was lacquered wood, painstakingly recreated identical to Old Earth design, with thin metal tiles embossed with longevity symbols. The inside, however, was more modern, a mess of tables with instruments: the communal network a knot of virtual messages with cryptic reminders like "put more khi at G4" and "redo the connections, please", notes left by researchers to themselves and to each other.

He kept a wary eye on the room—two tables, loaded with instruments; a terminal, blinking forlornly in a corner; a faint smell he couldn't quite identify on the air:

charred wood, with a tinge of a sharper, sweeter flavour, as if someone had burnt lime or longan fruit. No threat that he could see; but equally, a slow, spreading silence characteristic of hastily emptied room.

"Is anyone here?" Suu Nuoc asked—superfluous, really. The network would have told him if there were, but he was too used to battlefields, where one could not afford to rely on its presence or its integrity.

"She's not here," *The Turtle's Golden Claw* said, slowly, patiently; an adult to a child. As if he needed another patronising highborn of the court... But she was his charge; and so, technically, was Grand Master Bach Cuc, the Citadel project being under the watchful eye of the military. Even if he understood next to nothing about the science.

"I can see that." Suu Nuoc's eye was caught by the door at the furthest end of the room: the access to the shielded chamber, gaping wide open, the harmonisation arch showing up as de-activated on his network access. No one inside, then.

Except... he walked up to it and peered inside, careful to remain on the right side of the threshold. Harmonisation arches decontaminated, made sure the environment on the other side was sterile; and the cleansing of extraneous particles from every pore of his skin was an unpleasant process he would avoid if he could. There was nothing; and no one; no virtual notes or messages, just helpful prompts from the communal network, offering to tell him what the various machines in the chamber did—pointing him to Grand Master Bach Cuc's progress reports.

Not what he was interested in, currently.

He had another look around the room. *The Turtle's Golden Claw* had said Grand Master Bach Cuc had vanished mid-call. But there was nothing here that suggested anything beyond a normal night, the laboratory deserted because the researchers had gone to bed.

Except...

His gaze caught on the table by the harmonisation arch. There was an object there, but he couldn't tell what it was because Grand Master Bach Cuc had laid her seal on it, hiding it from the view of anyone who didn't have the proper access privileges—a private seal, one that wouldn't vanish even if the communal network was muted. Suu Nuoc walked towards it, hesitating. So far, he had done Bach Cuc the courtesy of not using his accesses as an Official of the First Rank; hadn't broken into her private notes or correspondences, as he would have been entitled to. Long Quan would have called him weak—behind his back when he wasn't listening, of course, his aide wasn't that foolish—but he knew better than to use his accesses unwisely. There were those at the court that hadn't forgiven him for rising so high, so quickly; without years of learning the classics to pass the examinations, years of toiling in some less prestigious job in the College of Brushes until the court recognised his merit. They called him the Empress's folly—never mind his successes as a general, the battle of Four Stations, the crushing of the rebel army at He Huong, the successful invasion of the Smoke People's territory: all they remembered was that he had once slept with the Empress, and been elevated to a rank far exceeding what was proper for a former (or current) favourite.

But *The Turtle's Golden Claw* wasn't flighty, or likely to panic over nothing. Suu Nuoc reached out, invoking his privileged access—the seal wavered and disappeared. Beneath it was...

He sucked in a deep breath—clarity filling his mind like a pane of ice, everything in the room sharpened to unbearable focus; the harmonisation arch limned with cold, crystalline light, as cutting as the edges of a scalpel.

The seal had hidden five pellets of metal; dropped casually into a porcelain bowl like discarded food, and still smelling, faintly, of anaesthetic and disinfectant.

Mem-Implants. Ancestor implants. The link between the living and the memories of their ancestors: the repository of ghost-personalities who would dispense advice and knowledge on everything from navigating court intrigues to providing suitable responses in discussions replete with literary allusions. Five of them; no wonder Grand Master Bach Cuc had always been so graceful, so effortless at showing the proper levels of address and languages whatever the situation.

To so casually discard such precious allies—no, you didn't leave those behind, not for any reason.

But why would an abductor leave these behind?

"She wouldn't remove—" *The Turtle's Golden Claw* said. Suu Nuoc lifted a hand to interrupt the obvious.

"I need to know where the Grand Master's research stood. Concisely." There wasn't much time, and evidence was vanishing as they spoke. The ship would know that, too.

The Turtle's Golden Claw didn't make the mocking comment he'd expected—the one about Suu Nuoc being Supervisor of Military Research and barely enough mathematics to operate an abacus. "You can access the logs of my last journeys into deep spaces," she said, slowly. "I brought back samples for her."

Travel logs. Suu Nuoc asked his own, ordinary implants to compile every note in the room by owner and chronological order.

"Did Grand Master Bach Cuc know where the Citadel was?" he asked. That was, after all, what those travels were meant to achieve: *The Turtle's Golden Claw*, Bach Cuc's masterpiece, diving into the furthest deep spaces, seeking traces of something that had vanished many years ago, in a time when Suu Nuoc was still a dream in his parents' minds.

The Citadel of Weeping Pearls—and, with it, its founder and ruler, the Empress's eldest and favourite daughter, Bright Princess Ngoc Minh.

The Citadel had been Ngoc Minh's refuge, her domain away from the court after her last, disastrous quarrel with her mother and her flight from the First Planet. Until the Empress, weary of her daughter's defiance, had sent the Imperial Armies to destroy it—and the Citadel vanished in a single night with all souls onboard, never to reappear.

"There were... trace elements from orbitals and ships," *The Turtle's Golden Claw* said, slowly, cautiously; he had the feeling she was translating into a language he could understand—was it mindship stuff, or merely scientific language? "Images and memories of dresses; and porcelain dishes..." The ship paused, hovering before the harmonisation arch. "Everything as fresh as if they'd been made yesterday."

"I understood that much," Suu Nuoc said, wryly. He didn't know what arguments Grand Master Bach Cuc had used to sway the Empress; but Bach Cuc's theory about deep spaces was well known—about the furthest corners, where time flowed at different rate and folded back onto itself, so that the past was but a handspan away—so that the Citadel, which had vanished without a trace thirty years ago, could be found in the vastness of space.

If you were a mindship, of course; humans couldn't go in that deep and hope to survive.

"Then you'll understand why she was excited," *The Turtle's Golden Claw* said.

"Yes." He could imagine it—Grand Master Bach Cuc would have been cautious, the ship ecstatic. "She thought you were close."

"No," *The Turtle's Golden Claw* said. "You don't understand, Book of Heaven. There were a few analyses to run before she could pinpoint a—a location I could latch on.

But she thought she had the trail. That I could plunge back into deep spaces, and follow it to wherever the Citadel was hiding itself. She thought she could find Bright Princess Ngoc Minh and her people."

Suu Nuoc was silent, then, staring at the harmonisation arch.

He wasn't privy to the thoughts of the Empress anymore; he didn't know why she wanted Bright Princess Ngoc Minh back.

Some said she was getting soft, and regretted quarrelling with her daughter. Some said she wanted the weapons that Bright Princess Ngoc Minh had designed, the technologies that had enabled the citadel to effortlessly evade every Outsider or Dai Viet battalion sent to apprehend her. And still others thought that the Empress's long life was finally running to an end, and that she wanted Ngoc Minh to be her heir, over the dozen daughters and sons within the Purple Forbidden City.

Suu Nuoc had heard all of those rumours. In truth, he didn't much care: the Empress's will was absolute, and it wasn't his place to question it. But he had listened in enough shuttles and pavilions; and his spies had reported enough gossip from poetry club competitions and celebratory banquets, to know that not everyone welcomed the prospect of the princess's return.

Bright Princess Ngoc Minh had been blunt, and unpleasant; and many had not forgiven her for disregarding her mother's orders and marrying a minor station-born; and still others didn't much care about her, but thought she would disrupt court life—and thus threaten the privileges they'd gained from attending one or another of the princes and princesses. One was not meant, of course, to gainsay the Empress's orders; but there were other ways to disobey...

"Book of Heaven?"

Suu Nuoc swallowed past the bile in his throat. "We must report this to the Empress. Now."

The Engineer

Diem Huong had been six when the Citadel of Weeping Pearls had vanished. Her last, and most vivid memory of it was of standing on the decks of one of the ships—Attained Serenity, or perhaps Pine Ermitage—gazing out at the stars. Mother held her hand; around them, various inhabitants flickered in and out of existence, teleporting from one to another of the ships that made up the city. Everything was bathed in the same cold, crisp air of the Citadel—a feeling that invigorated the bones and sharpened the breath in one's lungs until it could have cut through diamonds.

"It still stands," Mother said, to her neighbour: a tall, corpulent man dressed in robes of indigo, embroidered with cranes in flight. "The Bright Princess will protect us, to the end. I have faith..."

Diem Huong was trying to see the stars better—standing on tiptoe with her arms leaning on the bay window, twisting so that the ships of the Citadel moved out of her way. Thuy had told her that, if you could line things up right, you had a view all the way to the black hole near the Thirtieth Planet. A real black hole—she kind of hoped she'd see ships sucked into it, though Thuy had always been a liar.

The man said something Diem Huong didn't remember; Mother answered something equally unintelligible, though she sounded worried. Then she caught sight of what Diem Huong was doing. "Child, no! Don't shame me by behaving like a little savage."

It had been thirty years, and she didn't know—not anymore—which parts of it were true, and which parts she had embellished. Had she only imagined the worry in Mother's voice? Certainly there had been no worry when she and Father had boarded the ship back to the Scattered Pearls orbitals—enjoy your holiday, Mother had said, smiling and hugging them as if nothing were wrong. I will join you soon.

But she never had.

On the following morning, as they docked into the Central orbital of the Scattered Pearls, the news came via mindship: that the Citadel had vanished in a single night with all its citizens, and was nowhere to be found. The Empire's invading army—the soldiers tasked by the Empress to burn the Citadel to cinders—had reached the designated coordinates, and found nothing but the void between the stars.

Not a trace of anyone aboard—not Mother, not the Bright Princess, not the hermits—everyone gone as though they had never existed.

As time went on, and the hopes of finding the Citadel dwindled, the memory wavered and faded; but in Diem Huong's dreams, the scene went on. In her confused, fearful dreams, she knew every word of the conversation Mother had had; and every single conversation she had ever listened to—playing with her doll Em Be Be on the floor while Mother cooked in her compartment, with the smell of garlic and fish sauce rising all around them, an anchor to the childhood she had lost. In her dreams, she knew why Mother had chosen to abandon them.

But then she would wake up, her heart in her throat, and remember that she was still alone. That Father was never there; drowning his sorrows in his work aboard a merchant ship, coming home from months-long missions stupefied on fatigue, sorghum liquor, and Heaven knew what illegal drugs. That she had no brother or sister; and that even her aunts would not understand how crushingly alone and frightened she was, in the darkness of her cradle bed, with no kind words to banish the nightmares.

After a while, she started adding her own offerings to the ancestral altar, below the hologram of Mother, that treacherous image that would never change, never age; her tacit admission that Mother might not be dead, but that she was as lost to them as if she had been.

But that didn't matter, because she had another way to find the answers she needed.

Thirty years after the Citadel disappeared, Diem Huong woke up with the absolute knowledge that today was the day—and that, whatever she did, the trajectory of her life would be irrevocably altered. This time, it would work: after Heaven knew how many setbacks and broken parts. She wasn't sure where that certainty came from—certainly not from her trust in a prototype made by a handful of half-baked engineers and a disorganised genius scientist in their spare time—but it was within her, cold and unshakeable. Perhaps it was merely her conviction that she would succeed: that the machine would work, sending her where she needed to be. *When* she needed to be.

She did her morning exercises, flowing from one Piece of Brocade to the next, effortlessly—focusing on her breath, inhaling, exhaling as her body moved through Separating Heaven and Earth to Wise Owl Gazing Backwards; and finally settling on her toes after the last exercises, with the familiar, energised feeling of sweat on her body.

They didn't have a lab, of course. They were just private citizens with a hobby, and all they'd managed to get hold of on the overcrowded orbital was a deserted teahouse, cluttered with unused tables and decorative scrolls. Lam, always practical, had used some of the celadon drinking cups to hold samples; and the porcelain dishes with painted figures had turned out to withstand heat and acid quite nicely.

The teahouse was deserted: not a surprise, as most of the others were late risers. In the oven—repurposed from the kitchen—she found the last of the machine's pieces, the ceramic completely hardened, the bots scuttling onto the surface to check it withdrew as she reached for it. The etching of circuits was perfect, a silvery network as intricate as woven silk.

Diem Huong turned, for a moment, to look at the machine.

It wasn't much to look at: a rectangular, man-sized frame propped with four protruding metal struts, reminiscent of a high-caste palanquin with its all-but-obsolete bearers. They had used tables and chairs to get the materials; and some of the carvings could still be seen around the frame.

It had a roof, but no walls; mostly for structural reasons: all that mattered was the frame—the rods, cooled below freezing temperature, served as anchors for the generated fields. A lot of it was beyond her: she was a bots-handler, a maker and engraver of circuits on metal and ceramic, but she wasn't the one to design or master the machine. That was Lam—the only scientist among them, the holder of an Imperial degree from the prestigious College of Brushes, equally at ease with the Classics of Mathematics as she was with the Classics of Literature. Lam had been set for a grand career, before she gave it all up and came home to take care of her sick father—to a small, insignificant station on the edge of nowhere where science was just another way to fix failing appliances.

The machine, naturally, had been a welcome challenge to her. Lam had pored over articles from everywhere in the Empire; used her old networks of scientists in post in various branches of the Imperial Administration, from those designing war mindships to the ones on far-flung planets, tinkering with bots to help the local magistrate with the rice harvest. And, somehow, between all their late-night sessions with too much rice wine and fried soft crabs, between all their early-morning rushes with noodle soup heavy and warm in their bellies, they had built this.

Diem Huong's fingers closed on the piece. Like the previous one, it was smooth: the etchings barely perceptible, the surface cold. Would it be unlike the previous one, and hold the charge?

She knelt by the machine's side, finding by memory and touch the empty slot, and gently slid the piece into its rack. She could have relied on the bots to do it—and they would have been more accurate than her, to a fraction of measure—but some things shouldn't be left to bots.

Then she withdrew, connected to the room's network, and switched the machine on.

A warm red light like the lanterns of New Year's Eve filled the room as the machine started its warm-up cycle. She should have waited, she knew—for Lam and the others, so they could see what they had laboured for—it wasn't fair to them, to start things without their knowledge. But she needed to check whether the piece worked—after all, no point in making a ceremony of it if the piece snapped like the previous one, or if something else went wrong— as it had done, countless times before.

Put like that, it almost sounded reasonable. But, in her heart of hearts, Diem Huong knew this wasn't about tests, or being sure. It was simply that she had to see the machine work; to be sure that her vision would come to fruition.

The others wouldn't have understood: to them, the Citadel of Weeping Pearls was an object of curiosity, the machine a technical challenge that relieved the crushing boredom of mining the asteroid fields. To Diem Huong, it was her only path to salvation.

Mother had gone on ahead, Ancestors only knew where. So there was no way forward. But, somewhere in the starlit hours of the past—somewhere in the days when the Citadel still existed, and Bright Princess Ngoc Minh's quarrel with the Empress was still fresh and raw—Mother was still alive.

There was a way *back*.

The temperature in the room plummeted. Ice formed on the rods, became slick and iridescent, covered with a sheen like oil—and a feel like that of deep spaces permeated the room, a growing feeling of wrongness, of pressures in odd places the body wasn't meant to have. The air within the box seemed to change—nothing obvious, but it shimmered and danced as if in a heat-wave, and the harmonisation arch slowly revved up to full capacity, its edges becoming a hard blue.

"Up early?"

Lam. Here? Startled, Diem Huong turned around, and saw her friend leaning against the door, with a sarcastic smile.

"I was—" she said.

Lam shook her head. Her smile faded; became something else—sadness and understanding, mingled in a way that made Diem Huong want to curl up in a ball. "You don't need to explain."

But she did. "I have to—"

"Of course you do." Lam's voice was soft. She walked into the laboratory; stopped, looking at the machine with a critical frown. "Mmm."

"It's not working?" Diem Huong asked, her heart in her throat.

"I don't know," Lam said. "Let me remind you no one's tried this before."

"I thought that was the point. You said everyone was wrong."

"Not in so many words, no." Lam knelt by the rods, started to reach out a hand; and changed her mind. "I merely said some approaches had no chance of working. It has to do with the nature of deep spaces."

"The mindships' deep spaces?"

"They don't belong to the mindships," Lam said, absent-mindedly—the role of teacher came to her naturally, and after all, who was Diem Huong to blame her? Lam had built all of this; she deserved a little showing off. "The ships merely... cross them to get elsewhere? Space gets weird within deep spaces, that's why you get to places earlier than you should be allowed to. And where space gets weird, time gets weird too."

She called up a control screen: out of deference to Diem Huong, she displayed it rather than merely keeping it on her implants. Her hand moved in an ever-quickening dance, sliding one cursor after the other, moving one dial after the next—a ballet of shifting colours and displays that she seemed to navigate as fast as she breathed, as utterly focused and at ease as Diem Huong was with her morning exercises.

Then she paused; and left the screen hanging in the air, filled with the red of New Year's lanterns. "Heaven help me. I think it's working."

Working. Emperor in Heaven, it was working. Lam's words—she knew what she was talking about—made it all real. "You think—" She hardly dared to imagine. She would see the Citadel of Weeping Pearls again—would talk to Mother again, know why she and Father had been abandoned...

Lam walked closer to the harmonisation arch, frowning. Without warning, she uncoiled, as fluid as a fighter, and threw something she held in her hand. It passed through the door—a small, elongated shape like a pebble—arched on its descent downwards; and faded as it did so, until a translucent shadow settled on the floor—and dwindled away to nothing.

On the display screen, a cursor slid all the way to the left. Diem Huong looked at Lam, questioningly. "It's gone back? In time?"

Lam peered at the display, and frowned again. "Looks like it. I entered the time you gave me, about ten days before the Citadel vanished. " She didn't sound convinced. Diem Huong didn't blame her. It was a mad, unrealistic adventure—but then, the Citadel had been a mad adventure in the first place, in so many ways, a rebellion of Bright Princess Ngoc Minh and her followers against the staidness of court life.

A mad, unrealistic adventure—until it had vanished.

Lam walked back to the display. Slowly, gently, she slid the cursor back to the right. At first, Diem Huong thought nothing had happened; but then, gradually, she saw a shadow; and then a translucent mass; and then the inkstone that Lam had thrown became visible again on the floor of the machine, as sharp and as clearly defined as though it had never left. "At least it's come back," Lam said. She sounded relieved. "But..."

Back. So there was a chance she would survive this. And if she didn't—then she'd be there, where it mattered. She'd have her answers—or would, once and for all, stop feeling the shadow of unsaid words hanging over her.

Diem Huong moved, as though through thick tar—the gestures she had been steeling herself to make since this morning.

"Lil'sis?" Lam asked, behind her. "You can't—"

Diem Huong knew what Lam would say: that they weren't sure. That the machine was half-built, barely tested, barely run through its paces. For all she knew, that door opened into a black hole; or in the right time, but into a vacuum where she couldn't breathe, or on the edge of a lava field so hot her lungs would burst into cinders. That they could find someone, or pay someone—or even use animals, though that would be as bad as humans, really, other living souls. "You know how it is," Diem Huong said. The door before her shimmered blue; and there was a wind on her face, a touch of cold like the bristles of a brush made of ice.

Answers. An end to her nightmares and the fears of her confused dreams.

"I've known, yes," Lam said, slowly. Her hands moved; her arms encircled Diem Huong's chest. "But that's no reason. Come back, lil'sis. We'll make sure it's safe, before you go haring off into Heaven knows what."

There was still a chance. Diem Huong could still turn back—if she did turn back, she would see Lam's eyes, brimming with tears—would read the folly of what she was about to do.

"I know it's not safe," Diem Huong said; and, gently disengaging herself from Lam's arms, stepped forward—into a cold deeper than the void of space.

IN THE VANISHERS' PALACE

*In a ruined, devastated world, where the earth is poisoned and
beings of nightmares roam the land...*

*A woman, betrayed, terrified, sold into indenture to pay her
village's debts and struggling to survive in a spirit world.*

*A dragon, among the last of her kind, cold and aloof but desper-
ately trying to make a difference.*

When failed scholar Yên is sold to Vu Côn, one of the last dragons
walking the earth, she expects to be tortured or killed for Vu Côn's
amusement.

But Vu Côn, it turns out, has a use for Yên: she needs a scholar to tutor
her two unruly children. She takes Yên back to her home, a vast, vertig-
inous palace-prison where every door can lead to death. Vu Côn seems
stern and unbending, but as the days pass Yên comes to see her kinder
and caring side. She finds herself dangerously attracted to the dragon
who is her master and jailer. In the end, Yên will have to decide where
her own happiness lies—and whether it will survive the revelation of Vu
Côn's dark, unspeakable secrets...

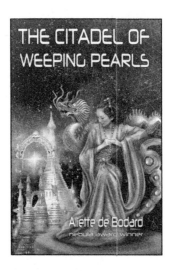

THE CITADEL OF WEEPING PEARLS

A Finalist for the 2015 Locus Award for Best Novella

The Citadel of Weeping Pearls was a great wonder; a perfect meld between cutting edge technology and esoteric sciences—its inhabitants capable of teleporting themselves anywhere, its weapons small and undetectable and deadly.

Thirty years ago, threatened by an invading fleet from the Dai Viet Empire, the Citadel disappeared and was never seen again.

But now the Dai Viet Empire itself is under siege, on the verge of a war against an enemy that turns their own mindships against them; and the Empress, who once gave the order to raze the Citadel, is in desperate needs of its weapons. Meanwhile, on a small isolated space station, an engineer obsessed with the past works on a machine that will send her thirty years back, to the height of the Citadel's power.

But the Citadel's disappearance still extends chains of grief and regrets all the way into the fraught atmosphere of the Imperial Court; and this casual summoning of the past might have world-shattering consequences...

THE OBSIDIAN AND BLOOD TRILOGY

Servant of the Underworld
Harbinger of the Storm
Master of the House of Darts

Year One-Knife, Tenochtitlan the capital of the Aztecs. Human sacrifice and the magic of the living blood are the only things keeping the sun in the sky and the earth fertile.

A Priestess disappears from an empty room drenched in blood. It should be a usual investigation for Acatl, High Priest of the Dead--except that his estranged brother is involved, and the the more he digs, the deeper he is drawn into the political and magical intrigues of noblemen, soldiers, and priests-and of the gods themselves...

"Amid the mud and maize of the Mexica empire, Aliette de Bodard has composed a riveting story of murder, magic, and sibling rivalry."
                    —*Elizabeth Bear, author of* All the Windwracked Stars

FOR NEWS ABOUT JABBERWOCKY BOOKS AND AUTHORS

THANKS FOR READING!

Printed in Great Britain
by Amazon